REALM OF DEMONS

THE DESERT CURSED SERIES, BOOK 9

SHANNON MAYER

HiJinks

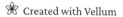 Created with Vellum

Acknowledgments

This book was a beast in all the ways it could be. I hope you enjoy the last ride with Zam, Maks and Lila as they (hopefully) get the HEA that you've all been waiting for. I say hopefully, because sometimes characters don't go quiet, even after the story is done.

I want to thank my amazing team, editors, proofers, Beta readers, author peeps, and my trusty as ever, bottle of Aleve. I could not have gotten through this book without you.

ONE

Nico

Two demons stood staring at the one they hoped would help them get to Asag. She stood on the beach, an array of shifters spread out in front of her with a herd of unicorns milling about.

Exactly as planned.

"That complicates things," Soleil sighed. "Why would she put her family in danger if she loved them? Asag's demons will not spare them."

Nico barely gave her a glance, though she was easily the most beautiful demon in all the realms, whether on this side of the Veil or the other. He tried not to think about her in that way. Not anymore.

"Maybe she didn't call them. She is rather independent."

That many unicorns, though . . . that would make things easier.

"They will suffer even more if she dies in front of them." Soleil looked away from the reunion. Nico tried to ignore the pain that vibrated off her. He knew pain well; it was one of his one gifts, and he used it well to his advantage. Soleil let out a slow breath, her wingtips nearly brushing his with the subtle movement. "There is not much more we can do to help."

"True." He scratched at one of his horns. "True. We have given her and that mate of hers all the chances we could when it comes to life and death." He knew what she was asking. One more time. Could they help her one more time? The rules were clear: they could not, and they both knew it. They could not bring her back from the brink of death if she fell to the darkness once more.

Even though she was so very close to reaching Asag, closer than anyone else had ever come.

"As long as we don't stop her from being killed . . . I do believe that was what was written."

He smiled and snapped the claw-tipped fingers on one hand. A scroll materialized in front of them both. The contract made between Asag and the demon realms. The silvery material unfurled, smoke rolling from where the words appeared across it.

He frowned as he saw the one name he hated more than any other appear.

Soleil's son had done more damage than Nico had ever thought possible. All because of a perceived slight against his mother. Nico snorted to himself.

His eyes drifted down to the last section. "There." He pointed at the paragraph. "Three times may the life of any challenger or their teammates be saved by another demon for any reason they see fit, whether to harm or help Asag."

Soleil frowned. "We have done that; we have helped them three times. So we are—"

"We are not saving her life if we give her a direction," Nico said.

His former wife looked at him, delicate brows furrowing. "The others, they would stop us."

"Not if we were in another's form." He was warming to the idea. "A body near death would be easy for us to take for a short time. None of the other demons would recognize us then."

Soleil's wings brushed across his back as she joined him at the lookout. He stifled a shiver of desire that nearly derailed his mind. He'd thrown away his kingdom once for her; he would not be so foolish as to do it again.

"Your plan . . . she would not trust us. They know what we are now. We must reach him, Nico. Or our world is lost. The realm is falling apart because of this breach between the two. It must be healed."

Yes, pain, the pain of a mother was exquisite, there was nothing quite like it. He closed his eyes to keep from feeding off her pain as he once would have. She was working with him now, he did not need to piss her off. He cleared his throat and waved a hand at the shifters and their unicorns. "As I said, we need bodies, or at the very least one body. Who would make a deal with a demon? Not one of them. They are all too . . ."

"Aware." Soleil nodded. "The girl and her mate, they know about us. I have a feeling that he . . . spoke with a hunter."

Nico tapped his claws on the rock, scratching out little gouges. "Roshawn?"

"Likely. The boy carries his blood. It would make the most sense. Roshawn was there, when Asag was bound. He might try to take the boy's body as his own."

"To think that we saved one of Roshawn's is galling, to say the least." Nico couldn't help the bitterness in his voice. "But that does not mean he will stay alive forever."

Soleil laid a hand on his shoulder, her warmth sinking through him. Just as he'd refused to swallow the pain, he would not allow himself to be comforted by her. That was not what they were any longer. This bargain they'd struck was for one reason only.

To save the demon realm.

"We need them to blaze the path to Asag. He has

been chained for far too long. We need to take him home."

She didn't take her hand from his shoulder.

Nico stared past the reunion on the beach. "Asag . . . has done much damage. I wish that we could just . . ."

"Kill him," Soleil said softly, at last removing her hand. Did she finally understand he could never turn to her like that again? Did she even realize she'd spoken those words out loud? Surely she did not still hate Asag?

"We cannot," he growled and lifted himself so he perched on the rock ledge as the monster he was, "or the demon realm would be destroyed. We must continue to find our way to my son. We can do this, Soleil. This is our best and perhaps only chance. Never before has anyone not only breached the challenges, but actually brought with them what was needed to break Asag's chains."

Chains that both held him captive here, and yet also kept him from returning to the demon realm.

Her swallow was audible. "And if Lilith is involved? What then? Your daughter would destroy—"

"She will die." Nico's face hardened as he lied through his teeth. "She will die, and I will cast her into the demon realm to do the killing myself."

His former wife didn't look away from him. They had for years lied to one another, did she suspect that his end game was different than hers?

No, she was too trusting, even now.

"Then we must find a body that we can convince to take at least one of us," Soleil said. "And fast. One that Zamira and her mate will trust, if such a thing is available."

Her wings spread and she let herself tumble off the rocks. Not that they truly stood there in the flesh; no, they existed in the in-between. In between the world and the demon realm. In between the world and the dreamscape. No one could see or hear them. Slipping through a crack that opened as the demon realm shattered from within, they had managed to find their way to this place of limbo.

They had not been called to this world and so they could not truly affect it. Not yet.

Nico watched her fly for a moment, letting himself remember what it was to be with her, to own her body, to see her smile turn his way, to feel her touch and to know that she'd chosen him above any other demon.

Those times were done, though. He knew that she wished to heal the demon realm, and she believed that he was going to help her.

But that was not what he was here for.

Shaking what remained of his feelings off, he spread his monstrous red leathery wings and fell from the rocks. They flew side by side toward the beach, their wingtips brushing over the people there, not even fluttering their hair.

Zamira was the only one who noticed them.

Frowning, she turned toward them for the split second that they passed her by.

That one was trouble. Nico knew it in his gut that it was a dangerous game Asag played with this shifter. For all those who'd tried to end Asag, this one was different. He could feel her bloodlines stretching out across the different species, and that made her unpredictable. It was best that she was unable to reach her own power.

That was a particularly clever trap that Asag had set.

"Where shall we look?" he called over the wind.

"There was a shifter that rode with her mate across the desert. He was lost when the Storm Queen took the Jinn," Soleil called back to him. "I don't believe he will be far."

She was not wrong.

The one they sought *wasn't* far, but he was well hidden, his heart rate difficult to pick up on as it stuttered and slowed. Hours ticked by before they found him. But he would be perfect for what they needed. He lay in the sand, under a thorn bush, skin torn, body frail, sobbing as though his heart was breaking.

"Heat madness." Soleil landed next to the rocking man, circling him carefully. "That will make it easy for you to take him."

Nico didn't disagree. "If he dies while I am in him . . ." They would be spun straight back to the demon realm. It had taken a long, long time and great patience to escape that realm, even to get to this in-between. He was not sure they would have another chance.

"He won't die, I don't think. He is heartbroken, injured, but far enough from death that we should be able to take safety in him." Soleil dropped next to the sobbing man. Spreading her wings wide, she tipped her head back and pulled the power of the sun into her until she began to glow, her image appearing in the corporeal world.

Fallen angel, she was that still. Her compassion was her undoing every time—as it had been his once. He shook his head again as the dark-haired, green-eyed man lifted his face to her beauty.

"My daughter," he whispered. "I see her in my dreams. I see her with the Beast from the East. This . . . how did this happen?"

"I will take you to her," Soleil whispered, brushing her wings across his face. "But you must take me and my mate with you."

The man held up his hands, palms toward Soleil. "Anything for my Reyhan."

CHAPTER
TWO

ZAMIRA

T he feeling of wing tips brushing across my face had me turning to the sky, even while my brother, his wife and the others of our shifter pride threw questions at me.

Was I okay?

Was there a battle to be fought?

What should they do?

"Zam," Bryce barked my name. "Are you listening?"

I lowered my eyes from the sky, even though I'd thought, just for a moment, I'd seen something there above us. A glimmer of wing tips?

I reached a hand for my brother and pulled him into a hug. He smelled like home, like the musk of lions and desert, like sand and the heat that baked the world I knew. I held onto him for perhaps longer than he'd thought I should, and finally he just held me out at arm's length.

"I am listening," I said. "I didn't want you to come; I was injured, but I am okay now. It seems that the world has other plans."

I truly did not want them here. With every fiber of my being, I wanted Bryce to take the pride and run. Take the unicorns and run. Even though the Storm Queen was dead and gone, and the threat to the unicorns dead with her, their arrival had me uneasy. Sick to my stomach.

He snorted and looked me over, his nose wrinkling as he took me in. "You look like shit. You know that, right?"

Lila leapt from Maks's shoulder over to mine and she hissed at Bryce. "Come, gentlemen, I hope we shall drink down all this unkindness. Or I'll kick your ass myself."

I reached up and tugged her tail. "It's okay, Lila. That's what brothers do. They state the obvious, because they're rarely smart enough to realize that stating the obvious is likely to get them a punch in the mouth. Or an ass-kicking from a dragon."

Maks leaned in close. "*Merry Wives of Windsor*, Lila."

"Damn it!" she grumbled. "I thought I'd have you on that one, Toad."

Bryce's smile was tight, restrained. "Yes, brothers are something like that. You look run-down, Zam. Like you've just come out of a battle." He held a hand up to Lila. "Is that more acceptable?"

She huffed and smacked his hand with the tip of her tail. "Barely."

I let him go and went to Kiara next. She held me tight. "Sister," she whispered. "We felt you dying. Are you truly okay?"

I breathed out a sigh. "It was temporary."

She gave me another squeeze. "We're here, we are with you doing whatever it is that you need to do this time. We aren't leaving."

The thing was, I believed her. I knew it to the marrow of my soul that my family had my back. Sure, my brother could be a dick (but let's be honest, a great deal of creatures with testicles had that tendency, which was why Balder was such a gem) but he had my back when the crunch time came.

And I had his.

Balder stuffed his nose into my hands and I cupped his muzzle, bringing his nose to my lips. "My friend, you found them out in the desert? Is that why you took off so easy when the golems came? They were why you didn't fight to stay by my side?" Not that I'd wanted him to, but every other time I'd sent him away, it had been difficult. This last time he'd taken off like a damn explosion had lit under his ass.

He breathed out and flicked his ears back and forth. And he winked one eye. I was sure it was because he'd sensed the pride getting closer on the backs of the rest of the unicorns. He'd know his family was drawing closer, just as I'd known mine was.

The little black mare that had carried Reyhan was next to greet me, but Maks beat me to her. "Queen, how did you make it back here?"

I turned to him. "You know her?"

"I traded Batman for her." The catch in his voice said it all. Letting go of the old black gelding had not been easy. Leaving a friend behind never was. "He couldn't keep going. And Balder had picked her out."

I slid my hand into his and gave his fingers a squeeze. I understood how hard it would have been to leave Batman behind. "Maybe we'll go back for him? To the trader?"

Maks squeezed my hand back. "Yeah, after this."

After this.

After we dealt with the demon known as the Beast from the East. Asag. After we survived that encounter.

With Balder and Queen with us, we had a chance now to fix at least one of my mistakes.

"We have to try to catch Reyhan," I said, pulling myself up onto Balder's back. "We can't leave her with the aqrabuamelu, and they can't have gone far. We can still catch them."

In one swift move gone so very wrong, she'd been taken away from us—essentially taking my place. The scorpion stinger that had hung around my neck and would teleport me to the aqrabuamelu and from there to Asag, the one I'd planned to put on the Storm Queen . . . Reyhan had put it around her own neck instead. My guts clenched, seeing it all over again.

Fen holding tight to her neck, Reyhan whispering that she was sorry. My jaw ticked as my throat tightened.

Maks jumped up onto Queen. "You know where she is?"

I didn't want to try and explain yet that it was my fault that she'd been taken. The scorpion stinger had dug into her flesh, transporting her to the aqrabuamelu: a giant scorpion with the upper body of a man attached to the torso, several stories tall. He'd been somewhat reasonable, letting me go, but it had been with a catch.

Someone had to be stung by the scorpion tail necklace as the sun set. Maks hadn't known that part of the deal.

"What about us?" Bryce said. "What can we do to help while you're gone?"

I looked at Pazuzu. "Fill them in on what we've been doing. We'll be back as soon as we can."

The rhuk fluttered her feathers, dancing across the sand. "Can I help? I like the little one."

"Pace us," I said. "I don't want to hurt the aqrabuamelu unless he won't give her up. He isn't truly one of the bad guys. Just stuck, like everyone else, by Asag and his fucking games."

At least, that's what he—Steven—had said, and I had no reason to doubt him seeing as he'd offered me a way out of being taken to the demon.

"Does the aqrabuamelu have a name?" Lila asked.

I grimaced as Balder leapt forward under me, my heels pressing into his sides. "Take a guess."

Lila tightened her hold on me as Balder galloped along. "No, you have got to be kidding me!"

"Yup."

Maks burst out laughing. "Steve?"

"Close," I yelled. "Steven."

Lila groaned. "Well, the last Steve wasn't too bad. I mean . . . he tried to help."

She wasn't wrong about the rabisu leader who took the name of Steve. That being said, I wasn't giving any man with the moniker of Steve much wiggle room until they proved otherwise.

I urged Balder up and over the first sand dunes and stared out into the open space of the desert, fully expecting to see the massive scorpion ahead of us. Nothing, not even a whisper of the scorpion tail. Panic surged through me. "He's huge, we should be able to see him."

I reached for the threads that tied me to my family. My brother, Kiara, Shem and the others ranged out behind us. Reyhan was part of that family too and I could touch her connection to me. . . "She's . . . so far away," I whispered, knowing that wherever she was, she was already out of reach.

The sensation pulled me downward. "He's under the sand." Steven was after all a scorpion. He'd burrowed down deep in order to get back to Asag.

"What about Fen?" Lila clutched at me.

"He's right with her." I touched her side, feeling her fear for the other dragon that she did not want to admit she had feelings for. "He's with her, Lila. That's good. He can help protect her. He's smart and strong."

At least that was what I was hoping. That they would keep each other safe while we did all we could to get to them. I didn't want to think about what would happen . . . if Asag had his way. Bile rose through me, and I choked it back down. Giving way to the fear and the panic, the guilt and worry would get us nowhere fast. We had to focus on getting there to them above all else.

"What do we do?" Lila asked. "How do we get to them?"

I stared out over the desert, toward where Asag sat on his throne, thinking that he was safe. Thinking that no one would ever make it through his challenges.

"We take the fight to the Beast from the East, and we break into the city of demons to do it. That's all there is to it." I turned Balder away, even though my heart ached. We weren't leaving Reyhan, not at all. But there was no way we could get to her—at least not yet.

I rubbed at my left hand. The nerves within it tingled and danced and when I looked down, I took note of the fact that my skin seemed more translucent. I flexed my fingers. Sparkles of magic danced under my skin.

Was it that droplet of magic that had stayed with me? In freeing the source of all magic, a drop of it had stayed with me. Why, I had no idea. But the buzzing under my skin was a steady presence.

I swallowed hard. Whatever it was, I would use it to free Reyhan, and stop Asag. Once and for all the demon would be dealt with.

Flexing my hand, I could almost feel a sword pressed against my palm as the pull from a darker magic tugged at me. Nope, that was not good. Because the only sword I had on me was Lilith. And Lilith was a raging psychotic bitch—sister to Asag, and a demon in her own right—who of course couldn't be trusted. She was worse than my flail which had tried to suck my life away on a number of occasions. A thousand times worse.

And yet, I was stuck with her. Just sitting there on Balder's back, my body tensed, the pressure of said sword on my back a steady reminder of her presence. Almost as if the sword had shifted in order to get my attention.

I grimaced. "Knock it the fuck off, Lilith."

Lila hissed, Maks shot me a look and I shook my head. "It's fine. She just moved."

"I think you should leave her behind," Lila said. "Bury her deep in the sands."

I didn't disagree on one level but . . . "And who would pick her up? Someone that she could manipulate, possess, and then Lilith would be free in this world. That's worse than me lugging her around.

Maybe we can do for her what we did for the flail, and release her soul along with Asag."

Release as in kill them both at the same time. Listen, let me have my dreams, alright?

Trotting along, back toward the pride and Pazuzu, a groan spun us to the left.

"What now?" muttered Lila. I agreed with her, we did not need any more surprises.

Another long, low moan, and a delicate arm lifted, a flash of a gem on one finger, and a swath of red cloth sliding down to show the pale skin beneath.

In the sand, face down, skirts partially covered by sand, was the figure of a woman that I thought had been killed. How in the world had she survived?

"Mamitu?"

Maks reached the goddess of the desert first, leaping off the black mare, water flask in hand. He lifted Mamitu up, offering her some water, pressing the flask to her lips.

Her face was speckled with sand, but her eyes were bright despite how dishevelled the rest of her was. Lifting a hand, she managed to push the flask away. "No, no, you must not let me live. He can take me again if he realizes I'm not dead." Her eyes swept past Maks to me, and it felt like we were at the beginning of our journey, when the hyena had spoken to us and warned us of the Beast from the East. "You are so close, Zamira, guardian of the desert. Do not waver. The fear will be heavy, but you, the three of you can do this. I believe in you. You must take what you have brought with you . . . take it all . . ."

"Mamitu, please, anything that you can tell us will help." Lila hopped back and forth across my shoulders as she spoke. "Anything? A weakness that Asag has?"

"His weakness is simple, so simple and yet you could never guesssss . . ." Her breath slid out of her, a long 's' that was drawn out, and her eyes took on the distant look that only death provided as she stared blankly up at the sky.

"No," I whispered as I reached for her body, even as she turned to sand and slid out of her own clothes, joining the dune that we sat on. Nothing but her voluminous red skirts were left. That and the single ring she'd worn. A glimmer of silver and red, the stone was rough-shaped, held tight by silver tendrils to the main part of the ring.

"Ashes to ashes, dust to dust," Maks whispered. "She is safer than the rest of us by a long shot."

I nodded. Mamitu was at peace now, and we were still up shit creek without a paddle, and a hole in the boat as the water poured in. I scooped up her skirts and the ring and mounted Balder.

He turned his head back, nuzzling the skirts before blowing out a big snort. She'd been kind to him, to him and to us as best she could be considering how tied she was to Asag.

"Let's go. There is nothing we can do for her now."

Cassandra swooped over top of us. "The little one is gone?"

I held up my hand. "Cassandra, can you help us still?"

She landed on the sand next to us. The two horses stepped back to give her room. "The sky above the demon city and above Asag's castle is impassable. If I could fly you straight there, I would."

Lila bounced across my shoulders to land on Balder's neck. "Can you at least keep picking off the golems?"

The rhuk clapped her beak. "Yes, I will do that. There were a few around the city edges. I will go now and clear the spaces of them." She didn't wait for me to say anything more, just lifted off into the night sky.

"That will help," Maks said softly. "A great deal. The more golems she removes, the better."

Lila flexed her wings. "If I could shift bigger, you wouldn't need the rhuk's help."

I patted her back. "But until we have our abilities back, we do need her help. This is good. She'll help clear the path."

With that, we turned and rode back toward my family. Our family.

The herd of unicorns that had brought them in milled about, eyes watchful, horns catching the light of the stars above us. Night had fully fallen now, and with it a coolness trickled through the air. A few of the unicorns reached out and touched Balder on the side, but he didn't slow. He didn't so much as glance their way.

As if he were no longer a part of them. I patted his neck. I understood his position, to be part of a family, but always somewhat on the outskirts. Looking in and wondering where you fit.

Bryce had the Bright Lion Pride putting together a camp on the edge of the water, setting up tents and cookfires already, spots of light illuminating the night. He was a good leader, and the pride respected him. That at least had finally come to fruition—he'd always been destined to be alpha. At least in my mind.

"Be wary." I pointed out to the water. "There are things deep in the ocean that don't play nice. And sometimes they can reach onto shore."

That had his attention. "We'll set back another hundred feet. Put guards to watch all sides of the camp."

"Prudent." I slid off Balder's back and gave his neck another pat. I was here, but my mind and heart were already well ahead, thinking about Reyhan. Thoughts of her followed me as I took the ring of Mamitu's and on a whim set it on my own finger. The skirts, though . . . I found myself stuffing them into one of the saddlebags.

Keep Reyhan safe, Fen, please keep her safe. That was the only hope we had—that Fen would somehow keep her clear of the demon until we got to them. Until we rescued them and killed Asag.

"What can we do?" Kiara's voice pulled me around. I looked at the girl who'd inadvertently saved me from my first marriage, the girl who had become a woman I was proud to call part of my family.

"Maks, Lila and I will sneak into the city and see if we can't get close enough to get Reyhan out. That's the first thing. Once she and Fen are clear, we can regroup and tackle Asag."

Pazuzu cleared his throat. "You don't want to know what the last challenge is? The last test that you must complete?"

I made myself look at him. Not because he was foul, but because I almost didn't give a shit about another test, or even Asag. I just wanted to get Reyhan back, I wanted to save her, and screw the damn challenges. "Is it ridiculous?" Because yeah, the rest of them had been ridiculous. Stupid. Impossible.

"It is in line with all that you've been doing. Because it is yet another impossible task." His voice was . . . careful. "You must free the golden dragon."

I stared at him. "We are planning on freeing all the dragons anyway. Letting them go home to their families." Just as soon as Reyhan was safe.

He shook his head slowly. "More than that. The golden dragon is in a cage next to Asag himself. You must navigate the demon city of Trevalon, through to the castle, free the dragon and then, only then can you face Asag. Then you will be able to save the girl and your friend, Fen. The one thing that will open the cage is a unicorn horn, so you must take one with you." Pazuzu looked us over. "If it were anyone else, I would have no faith that they could achieve the impossible. But I am inclined to believe after all I've seen that if anyone can do this, it is you." He bowed from his waist to me. "I must wait here, Zamira. I cannot give you any other assistance."

Lila snorted and the ground sizzled with a bit of her acid. "Right, like that's a shocker?"

I stared at him. He and Mamitu had helped, but . . .just enough to make me feel like I was still very much on my own with my friends.

I held out my hand to Pazuzu. "What about your other friend? Should I not have to go to him first? Like I came to you and Mamitu?" Damn my brain, I could not remember his name.

Pazuzu shook his head. "You *are* going to him. He *is* the golden dragon. He can traverse the dreamscape to speak to us, but of the three of the guardians he is literally the most bound to Asag."

Maks held up a hand, drawing Pazuzu's eyes to him. "Is it a true cage, or something else, like a spell that binds the golden dragon to Asag?"

"Both." Pazuzu dipped his head toward Maks. "A collar and chain bind him to the throne, and a spell keeps him from being able to think as anything but an animal. He is trapped inside the body. And while it is actually one of his forms, he is still trapped. The unicorn horn you carry will free him."

Lila let out a slow whistle. "He's a dragon shifter?"

Pazuzu gave her a nod. "Yes. The last."

Lila's claws tightened on my shoulder, and her anxiety spiked through our connection. "Bad?" I asked.

"Just . . . dragon shifters are dangerous because they can literally be anything. A dragon, a wolf, a hyena . . ." Her eyes shot to mine at the same time that a gasp escaped me.

"Was there one other," I asked Pazuzu, then tried again, "Another dragon shifter, a female?"

Pazuzu looked straight at me. "Yes, his mate. She fled but was cursed to die if she tried to leave. She'd never dared before. She disappeared weeks ago. Why?"

It was my turn to share a look with Maks and then Lila. "We met her. She gave us a warning as she died."

Pazuzu closed his eyes. "Do not tell the golden dragon that his mate is dead. It will break what is left of his mind."

I wanted to ask how could he not know that his own mate was gone. But then, that was easy for me. I was connected to my loved ones in the way that alphas were connected to their prides, packs, or chosen family.

I backed away from Pazuzu. "Then we won't tell him. I'll let you have that honor when the time comes since he is your friend."

Lila grumbled something under her breath. "Let's just hope he doesn't ask, because you aren't much of a liar."

No, I wasn't much of a liar.

Balder bumped my elbow, his dexterous lips pulling at the sleeve of my cloak. I nodded. "I agree, it's time to go." Reyhan and Fen were depending on us. We had to get to them.

"Wait . . ." Bryce put a hand on my arm. "We are here to help you. You can't just leave! So tell us, sister, what would you have us do? How can we help?"

THREE

I looked my brother over, seeing the changes in him, seeing the growth and strength that had developed even just since I'd seen him last. He'd not always been a good person; pain and despair had made him miserable to even those he loved. Deep inside he'd always loved me. And I knew that.

Even if he had been a fucking dink most days.

The question was, did I need him and my family here, or did I just want the comfort of knowing we weren't alone? I closed my eyes and bowed my head to think.

The pride was strong, all of them good fighters, but against demons? Fuck. They didn't have magic. They didn't have special weapons like me.

"Go home." I spoke as I lifted my head. "Take the unicorns and ride out of here, tonight."

Gasps circled around the camp.

Pazuzu choked. "What? You can't send them home! It is part of the prophecy that an army—"

I held up a hand, cutting him off. "I don't want my family paying the price for this quest of ours. Maks, Lila and I chose to come here. We chose to find the dragons' young ones. Us. Not Bryce, not Kiara, not any of you."

I could feel the anger bubbling around in the pride now. "You think we're weak? That we can't fight?" someone from the back shouted.

I shook my head. "What I know is that this is *not* your fight. What I know is that our pride has done enough to protect and fight for our place in the desert. What you'd face . . . the demons, the golems, the monsters unknown, it is not something I'd wish on any of you. You are my family. And it is my job to protect you."

"And you are ours," Kiara said.

I smiled. "Which is why I am telling you it's time to go. It's time to leave."

The muttering was loud, and not at all happy. Bryce stared me down. "Many did not want to come, and now you're proving them right."

I had no doubt about that. "I didn't ask you to come, Bryce. I told you to stay away."

His face hardened. Yup, there was the fucking dink. "Fine."

"Fine," I threw back at him.

Pazuzu lifted his hands to the sky. "No, this cannot

happen, you must stay! She will not survive without you!"

Well that was . . . unexpected. Bryce paused. "My sister will do as she pleases. She always has and she has yet to die."

Pazuzu stood in front of Bryce. "A compromise then. There is a city, on the water's edge. Tomorrow, make your way there, split up, spread out. See if you can convince anyone to fight with us, against Asag, but do it carefully. Then you are not in the front lines. Would that be sufficient?" He looked at me first.

Fucking hell, I did not want my family anywhere near this city, Asag, his demons or whatever remained of the golems. "It is not. I want them gone." The more I thought about it, the more certain I was that Bryce, the unicorns, all of them were in danger.

BRYCE GAVE a quick nod to Pazuzu, ignoring me. "We'll find any shifters there first. And go from there."

He stared hard at me. "Don't die." That was the equivalent of *I love you, but I'm pissed at you right now.*

I stared right back. "You either. Again."

He grimaced and turned his back on me.

So much for getting my family to safety.

Of course, leaving wasn't going to be that easy. Because I hadn't seen my family in months and there was one more member of our pride who wanted to say hello so that he could say goodbye.

"Shem." I caught my crazy-as-a-mad-hatter uncle in a quick hug. "Unless you have something helpful, I don't have time to chat. Unless of course you have a way to make my idiot brother leave?"

His long, slim arms wrapped around me, and he held me tight. "I have nothing helpful; I don't think. But you need to know we will all come when you call. There is going to be a fight, yes?"

I looked up into his golden eyes, seeing the concern and love there for me. For all of us. "Yes, there is going to be a fight. But it is not one you or the others should be a part of."

"Then reach for us." He patted my cheeks as if I'd not just told him to get to safety. "You are not alone, Zamira of the Bright Lion Pride. You are never alone."

Kiara stepped up on the other side of him. "He's right. You can try all you want to send us away, but Bryce doesn't want to leave you here alone. Despite what he said," she said softly.

My jaw ticked as I held back the emotions and the tears that threatened at the backs of my eyes. My family loved me. Even if at times we'd fought and argued, they loved me. And in that love, I felt the hope that there was a chance we'd be able to pull this off, kill Asag, save Reyhan and all of us make it out unscathed.

Yup, I was delusional.

My chest got tighter yet, and hot, as though a fiery ember had landed against my skin. My hand tingled and I clenched it hard, my fingers digging in around the ring that had been Mamitu's.

Pazuzu's voice rang out over the group. "Five days from now, go to your sister."

Bryce and the other lion shifters faced Pazuzu. Bryce gave him a half bow from the waist. "Dawn on the fifth day, we ride to the city of demons, to show them our teeth."

A roar started in the back of the pride, and it was quickly picked up, a cheer that swelled around us. Instead of filling me with that hope that I'd felt a moment before, it filled me with dread.

Fear clawed at my throat. "Bryce, you have to go!" I yelled at him. He closed the distance between us, his face a storm cloud of anger and perhaps fear.

"I will not leave you. What kind of alpha would I be if I left you to die?"

I shoved him away from me. "The kind that understands you cannot sacrifice the one for the many."

Oh, that one stung. Words that our father had spoken time and time again. Bryce paled. I turned my back on him knowing that leaving him with those words were the best I could do to send him far from me. Far from this place.

"Let's go." I touched Maks on the hip and together we mounted up on Balder and Queen.

The roars of the lion pride chased us out of camp. Only then did I let the tears stream down my cheeks. Love had a funny way of doing that to me, making me cry even when it wasn't necessary. Or maybe it was just that this was all too much. I could feel death waiting to take out my family, and no amount of love would save them from the demons that waited.

I could only hope that our father's words would sting Bryce enough to send him away.

Lila sat on my shoulder and brushed her claws across my cheeks, catching the tears.

"My drops of tears I'll turn to sparks of fire," she whispered. "We are the fires that will burn him to the ground, Zam. I believe it. You did the right thing. They need to go."

Maks reached over and touched my arm. "I believe it too." He paused and yanked Lila's tail, pulling her off balance. "And it's *Henry VIII*, Lila, so nice try."

"Damn it, we were having a moment, Toad!" She launched at him, and he steered Dancer (apparently that was her name, not Queen as Reyhan had named her) away, laughing as she gave chase.

I dried my tears and looked over at them. Laughing, playing, loving—even in these darkest moments that we faced. *This* was worth fighting for, this was worth going to battle against an undefeated demon, his army, and a slew of dragons that were under his control.

No problem.

Some might think it callous to laugh when our friends—Reyhan, Fen, and all the stolen dragons—were in danger. But life had shown us we would not know when the moment would come that we'd look death in the eye and let it take our hand. So, you took the moments of joy with the moments of sorrow, to live your life to the hilt every day.

"Let's show them who's the fastest," I whispered to Balder. He leapt forward with a snort, and I urged him to take as much speed as he wanted. We passed Maks and Dancer in a flash and then they were galloping after us, Lila clinging to his shoulders, shrieking into the night.

We raced along the beach, heading toward the shoreline of the city that bordered the Sea of Storms. The sounds of wings had me tipping my head up.

The rhuk swooped through the darkness, nearly silent as they plucked up any of the golems remaining, dropping them out in the water.

"Thank you!" I shouted up at them.

I found myself glancing out at the rocky island keep that had belonged to the Storm Queen. I wondered how Vahab was doing with his new lady love. More than one rhuk could be seen out there, roosting for the night.

That made me smile. Vahab deserved whatever came his way. Even as I thought it, I frowned. Did he? He'd been trying to stop Asag too, even if each time the opportunity presented itself he was quick to leave his friends behind. But he'd faced Asag before, challenged him and lost. And now was trying to make it right.

"We might have to rescue him." I pointed out at the island. "After all this."

Maks's eyebrows shot up. "Rescue him? I thought he wanted to get baby making?"

"He was trying to stop Asag, the only way he knew how," I shouted into the wind. "He didn't want to flounce me, but he felt like he had to in order to fulfill the prophecy. I'm not happy about that, but I understand he didn't want to either."

Maks went from surprise to anger in a flash. "He tried to rape you?"

"I kicked his ass," Lila said. "But I think I see what Zam is trying to say. Vahab went about it all the wrong way, but he was trying to do the right thing. Just not well."

I pointed at her. "Exactly. But that doesn't mean I want to deal with him right now, we have enough shit —" Balder slid to a stop and reared up, cutting me off.

I clung to his back as he got himself situated and all four feet back on the ground.

A man I thought I'd never see again sat on the ground in front of us, nearly invisible in the dark of the night. It was a good thing that Balder had seen him, or we'd have trampled the man. Slim build, dark hair, dark skin, green eyes. He could have been my brother, or at least he looked more the part than Bryce with his blond hair and golden lion eyes. "Jasten?"

Maks grunted as if I'd punched him in the gut. "I'm

surprised to find you alive, friend. But happy to see you nonetheless."

Jasten slowly turned his green eyes to us. "I am still here, though I wonder how too. I was dying in the desert; I was sure of it. Run off, ignored by the rhuk that took you, my friend." He tipped his head toward Maks. "But now, here I am."

It took me a minute to put it together. I'd met Jasten outside the jungle of the rabisu. I'd found Reyhan within that same jungle. The pieces clicked together. "Reyhan is alive."

He just stared at me, blankly. "Who?"

I stared back at him. "I thought . . . you were looking for your wife and children when we met in the jungle. And after I sent you away, there was a little girl that I found hiding from the rabisu. Her name is Reyhan. Is she not yours?"

What were the chances that another child had been taken? I suppose fairly high considering the rabisu hunted the lands around their jungle.

He slowly shook his head. "No. Though a child surviving the jungle of the rabisu is amazing. I wish she were mine." He looked past me. "Where is she, this wondrous little survivor?"

I glanced at Maks. Was he picking up on the weirdness in the way that Jasten was speaking? Or was it just that I had not known him that long? How he was framing his words was . . . odd.

"Come." Maks reached down for Jasten. "You can

help us find our way through the outer city. You said that there was a way when we rode together." Maks glanced at me. "The plan had been to find a way in to Asag's city and wait for you there. Jasten had a way."

"I did, I did," he said, then let out a long sigh. "I did. I feel strange. Do I seem strange to you? Did I die?"

He let Maks help him and as he unfolded from the ground, his body looked as though it were indeed on the edge of death. "Lila, grab him something from the pack. Something to eat." I handed over my own water flask. "You aren't dead, my friend, and if you were this would surely be hell, not heaven."

Jasten took it and sucked down several gulps, murmuring his thanks to me and Lila as she handed him strips of dried meat. Most likely camel but could also be beef if Bryce had brought it with him. Apparently our saddlebags had been stocked full.

"With thanks," he said around a mouthful. "And yes, I will still help you. The city is as familiar to me as the back of my hand. As long as it has not changed since I was here last, I can help you. We will stop Asag."

He leaned against Maks's back and I found myself looking at my mate. His eyes were as full of the uncertainty I felt in my own.

This man looked and sounded like Jasten, but there was something wrong. Perhaps it was just the desert sickness that came with too much heat. Maybe something else?

Lila hopped across to me as we started out again and whispered in my ear, "He seems weird."

I nodded but kept my thoughts to myself. If he could help us get through the city, all the better.

We rode in silence the rest of the way, at a more moderate pace. The darkness of the night was our friend, keeping us from being easily seen. As we drew close to the outskirts of the city, the sand turned to a packed road. People moved along it both ways, to and from the desert and the docks, lanterns clutched in their hands. The night had fallen, but it was hardly beyond when others would be traveling. I found myself tugging my cloak hood up, and Maks did the same. We weren't the only riders on the road, but there weren't enough on horseback that we were going to disappear in the crowd.

"Did you hear?" an old, shrivelled woman on the side of the road called out, holding a torch in one hand and a dead bird by the wing. Her hair was short, white, and wild, sticking up in every direction. "The Storm Queen is with child!"

"That was quick," Lila muttered. "Vahab has some serious swimmers."

My lips twitched. "How did you come by this news?"

The old woman swung her gaze my way. Glittering black eyes swept over me and in them I saw a glimmer of a demon. Fuck.

"Ah, so the riders finally come again. The time is

nigh, the blistered gates will open, the city of Trevalon will fall. Heed me, thy time is nigh!" She left off with a cackle as she swept her long robes around her body and crouched down. I fully expected her to disappear, and I think she did too. She peeked up over her arm, only her eyes visible. "Get thee gone!"

"Does she think we can't see her?" Lila asked out the corner of her mouth.

I shrugged. "Doesn't matter. Thanks for the warning, old one."

I turned away from her, knowing that her warning was not unwarranted for those around us. There was a battle coming and they would be in the middle of it if they did not leave. But how to help them? I knew as well as Maks and Lila did that the one doing the warning would be the first to have stones cast at them. Especially because we were the outsiders. We were the trouble bringers.

I found myself looking at the other travelers. How many were demon-infested? How many were actual demons? I drew in a breath, looking for the scent that I associated with Asag.

It was fucking everywhere. Anxiety flowed through me. Time to move faster.

My heels bumped a little more against Balder's sides, and he picked up a trot. The road slid through an oversized brick gate that could easily have three wagons going through side by side. There were no guards that I could see.

The rhuk had done well getting rid of the golems.

Maybe there was no need for other guards? Maybe this was not the city that needed to be protected, being as close as it was to Asag.

At least that's what I thought. Night was fully upon us now and there were lights here and there, illuminating the streets, throwing shadows.

Maks took the lead as we stepped through the main gates. "Jasten, where can we rest that will be safe?"

"The big inn, it sits in the middle of town. Less likely to be noticed with all the comings and goings." He mumbled and touched his head. "Forget what it's called, big place, very big. I feel strange, Maks. Not myself. Do I have a fever still?"

Maks clapped a hand on his shoulder. "You've been out in the desert and fried your mind. A good sleep, some fluids, you'll be on the mend soon enough."

I nodded. "He's right. The sooner we get somewhere to hunker down, the sooner we can make a plan, the better this will be."

We wove our way through the town, heading for the center of it. I took note of the number of buildings, how close together they were, the number of vendors, and the number of homes—though whether or not anyone lived in them was debatable. Even though it was early in the night, there were no lights on inside most of the homes. They were dark and cold looking.

Through all that, I still hadn't seen any guards.

Maybe there were no other guards besides the golems? Somehow I doubted that and that truth only made my skin crawl and my fur want to puff up.

The other inhabitants—the few people we rode by —either had their heads down, ignoring us, or were incredibly nosy. Those that ignored us, acted as if we didn't exist. And those that didn't?

"Oy-a, who is you?" a man called to us from the shadows of a building, his pipe lighting up his face only a little.

"Travelers." Maks gave him a wave. "Stopping for the night."

"Oy-a, you headed east in the morning?" He flicked his pipe, sending embers to the ground.

Maks just nodded at him. Lila clung a little tighter to my neck. I didn't like the way the man's voice sounded. Warbling. And the smell that came from him was dark, rotten like death.

Lilith shivered and I took a bit of knowledge from her. She hissed at me, but I didn't care.

"Demon," I breathed out.

Yup, a demon. We kept on riding as if we weren't bothered, but my skin was crawling. How many demons were here? One was too many as far as I was concerned.

"Oy-ya!" he called after us. "You soft for this place."

"We'll be fine," Jasten called back. "Go back to sleep, Pearso."

My eyebrows shot up. How the hell did he know

that demon's name? Maks swept a quick look to me and I could see he had the same question.

A few others swept past us, none as nosy as Pearso.

"He's very cocky," I muttered to Lila. She was wrapped tight around my neck.

"Who? Pearso?"

I did another sweep of the area, noting the lack of . . . well, of anything that we should be running from or fighting. It made me itchy.

"Asag," I said softly. "It's like he's not afraid of anyone coming in. You'd think with a prophecy that is so long standing, that he'd at least safeguard himself against it?"

I mean, that seemed logical to me.

Lila flexed her tail and tucked her head in tight to mine. "Maybe we just aren't seeing the booby traps? Is that possible? He is a demon, it could be something out of our scope of knowledge."

She was right. But even so I found it unsettling, the lack of guards. The lack of a show of force after everything Asag had done to trap or kill us, depending on the day right up to this point.

"He likes to be entertained," Jasten said softly, his voice pitched . . . higher. More feminine. "Everything he does is so that he has a show to watch, a spectacle to amuse him in his castle."

"How do you know this?" Maks asked.

Jasten shook his head and cleared his throat, his

voice dropping back to a more normal register. "A guess."

Didn't sound like a guess to me. But I didn't press him, and neither did Maks. We were out in the open, Jasten was not well, and we had to get some sort of cover where we could make a plan.

Half an hour and we were standing in front of the oversized inn. It was five stories high and had lights in every window so that it shone like a beacon. No, really, literally shining so bright I had to cover my eyes, shading them with my hand.

I grimaced when I read the name. "*The Demon's Rest*. Really?"

"Safer here, where there are many, many . . . people . . . coming and going," Jasten pointed out. "I think that is what you want, yes? What we want."

It was, but the name could use some tweaking, I didn't need no resting demons here.

And I was not oblivious to the way he'd paused over the word 'people'.

I made myself draw in a deep breath through my nose, holding it at the back of my throat. Tasting it.

Dust.

Horses.

Leather.

Demons.

No scent of the average person anywhere. I swallowed hard.

Maks slid off Dancer and gave her a pat on the neck. "Let me go in, see what I can do."

Much as I hated that he was right to take the lead, I could still be irritated that a woman tromping about and asking for a room would be far more trouble than we needed. Lila hadn't moved from her spot where she'd tucked herself deep into my cloak, hiding from prying eyes.

"I know we are going to sleep here," she said softly, "but do we dare wait? Reyhan and Fen are with that monster."

I reached for the threads that tied them to me. They were scared, but not hurt. Maybe just put into a cell or something? I had no idea exactly what was happening. Only that they weren't dead, and they weren't injured.

"If we move when we are at our weakest, then we have less of a chance of saving them," I whispered back. "We have barely come off a fight with the Storm Queen and . . ." I didn't dare say Lilith's name out loud. Not here. "And the other who tried to make me her slave."

"Saving the girl?" Jasten asked softly. "You would risk your life for a child that was not your own. Interesting."

I shot him a look. Yeah, he was definitely off. "You risked your life for your own child, even knowing that it was unlikely she was alive in the forest of the rabisu. Why is it so hard to believe I'd fight for this one when we have a chance to save her?"

He shrugged. "It's not the goal that you set out with. The goal is to deal with . . ." He bobbed his head north. As if he knew where Asag's castle was. This was getting weirder and weirder.

Yeah, I didn't think saying Asag's name out loud was a good idea either. "Dealing with him is the goal, saving the dragons is the goal. But I won't leave my friends behind. We will deal with the . . . bad guy at hand, rescue our friends, rescue the other ones too."

Blah, I hated to curb my words. I wanted to fucking well say what I wanted to say out loud.

The door to the inn opened and Maks came out with a scrawny kid at his side. "This one will take care of the horses."

Jasten and I dismounted and the little guy took the horses' reins. "Come on, beautiful ones," he whispered to them. I drew in a breath and wrinkled my nose. The kid was a demon?

Before I could take the reins back, Balder bumped him with his nose and whuffled his unruly curls. I breathed a sigh of relief I hadn't realized that I'd been holding in. The horses would be safe for the night with the boy. I trusted Balder to make a good choice.

We took our saddlebags with us—there was no way I'd leave a unicorn horn just sitting out in the stables.

I clenched my hand. Mamitu's ring . . . the rock on it had slid around and was upside down, and dug into my palm.

Maks slid his arm around my waist. "I've got us a room, two beds, and dinner taken up to the room. We'll try to keep a low profile. Figure out things, leave early." He paused. "It's rough in there. I didn't see any women."

I gave his arm a squeeze. "If that's the case, Lila and I will go through the window. What floor?"

"Top, corner, on the side facing the palace," Maks said and turned so he gave me cover to shift.

Two men traveling together were even less notice-able than if I was involved—particularly if there were no other women in the inn. That was weird enough as it was. Normally the women were serving, or enter-taining. I handed him my saddlebags, then slipped into the shadows and stepped between the doorways in my mind, sliding down to four small paws. A small black house cat once more, I leapt up and grabbed at the downspout, using it to climb to the first roof line. Lila joined me, not flying but climbing along with me, her claws digging into the brick and wood easily.

"You think we're being watched?" she asked quietly.

"I think this whole city is being watched. I feel eyes on me, and there are fucking demons everywhere," I grumbled as I landed in front of a window. Even as I said the words, the sensation that eyes were on us grew heavier as though they'd focused on us even more. The people behind the window were arguing— all men. I kept on going, working my way up to the top floor, shoulders hunched. "That woman on the road, she could have been a spy for Asag. We don't know. She recognized us. Or at least she saw potential with the prophecy."

Lila climbed ahead of me, reaching the top first. "Maybe, but . . . look at the view . . . holy shit, Zam this is . . . this is a view."

I caught up to her and looked out to the north. The palace was in the distance, but what was between us and the palace was no small thing. The space, the very air, shimmered, as if it were made of clouds or fog.

The barrier closest to us was a twenty-foot wall that ran east and west, with a massive gate that looked to be the only way in. Beyond the wall was . . . hard to see. Between the dark and the fog that lay heavy on the space, I wasn't sure what was waiting for us.

"Lila, go grab the binoculars from Maks."

She shimmied down the roof to our room window and was back in a flash. I stepped between the doorway in my mind, back to two legs so I could take the binoculars. Adjusting myself on the roof, I lifted them to my eyes.

That didn't really improve what I was seeing. The palace was a little clearer. But based on the distance, it was easily a hundred miles. Sure, I could see it because the space between us and it was completely flat. But crossing to get there in five days? That was what Pazuzu had told Bryce to be ready for.

Fucker. My family being here just complicated my life. And gave me a perfect Achilles heel.

"Lila, if it was just a straight shot, no obstacles, Balder and Dancer could make the run in half a day, easily. Call me crazy, but I don't think it's going to be as simple as going for a hard gallop."

"Yeah, me neither." She crawled up across my knee. "Can you see them?"

"I'm looking."

I swept my view slowly left to right. Heat shimmered up around the base of the palace, as though the sands were still cooking from the sun. I stared, hoping to see something that would give me hope. Which was ridiculous, at this distance I wouldn't be able to see Reyhan or Fen. Did I think they'd be waving at me from the turrets? That I'd even be able to pick them out?

All I could do was look and wonder just how the fuck we were supposed to get to Asag and his palace. I lowered the binoculars and narrowed my eyes at the fog beyond the twenty-foot wall. "This, where we are, is not Trevalon, is it?" I said quietly. "I'd lay money that this is just the outskirts."

"I'm thinking that is," Lila pointed with the tip of her tail. "The big wall stretching as far as I can see east and west, it is kind of a giveaway. That and the sign."

I looked at where she pointed. An arched gateway made of . . . I stared hard, letting what I was seeing sink in. "Bones, it's made of bones. The wall too." Nice touch. Above the bone gate the letters of the city were burnt into the bleached bones. *Trevalon.* The way was not open through the gateway, but locked with a chain that shimmered with a magic even I could see at this distance. On either side of the gates stood four golems, just for good measure.

"Fuck," I whispered. "There is no way past those easily."

"Yeah. So how do we get into the city? Because that's where we have to go." Lila gripped the edge of the roof.

I looked again through the binoculars, sweeping the fog.

As the wind blew, the fog lifted here and there, giving me a glimpse of what lay beneath the mists. Buildings, lots and lots of buildings. Movement, bodies here and there. Demons maybe?

I swallowed hard. "This may be the worst thing we've faced yet," I said softly.

"Worse than your grandfather?" she asked.

"Yeah. Worse than that old bastard, or his son." I shook my head. "How do we get through that?" I waved at the space in front of us. "I mean, the distance is one thing, and if there are demons within the walls waiting on us . . . we could stay small, but I can feel the time ticking. The fastest thing would be to get that gate open for Bryce and the others and then we can all gallop straight to Asag."

As we watched, the thick fog shimmered and lightning danced in and out of it. Movement drew my eyes to the left center and then to the right center of the foggy city. The fog blew off and I lifted the binoculars. Dragons that had been still as statues lay in cages set up on poles within the city. Why?

"Dragons in cages, just to add to it," I said softly. Was that where Asag kept the hatchlings? Why?

Lila growled and shuddered. "This is bullshit."

I didn't disagree.

"How far from the gate to the doors of the castle?" Lila sat next to me and draped an arm across my thigh.

"Hundred miles, give or take. The flat plain makes it look closer. Like a mirage."

"What's that?" Lila climbed up to my shoulder and turned my head. I gasped as I watched the giant scorpion aptly named Steven appear out of the fog right at the edge of the shimmering sand, and head toward the castle. I couldn't see Reyhan, I couldn't see Fen, but I knew they were there.

Lila shot into the air. "I could fly there! I could snag them both!"

"No, the dragons! The golems!" I grabbed her tail and dragged her back down to sit next to me. "Lila, we will get them out, I promise you that. But not if we aren't smart about this. I'd like to get us all out in one piece. I can't risk you for them. That's not how this works."

The window below us cracked open and the smell of my mate flowed out along with the smell of food that had my stomach growling. Lila gave a whimper. I knew exactly how she felt. We were so very close, and yet so very far away.

"We'll get them out," I whispered. "Just let's see Asag try to stop us."

Yeah, I really shouldn't have tempted fate like that.

FOUR

Maks had done a good job in picking out the food. There was a garlic and onion hummus and a lovely soft bread for dipping into it, a shank of lamb for each of us, some sort of creamy sweetened rice, and a tankard of alcohol that Lila went straight to. She dipped her head into it.

"You found țuică!" she squealed and dove for the plum liquor. I slid through the window and plunked her out of the drink by the tail. "How about we wait till we get some food into you? I don't need you throwing up acid."

She grumbled, but then I dropped her onto the plate with the biggest shank of meat. She tore into the food. "Cooked. But I'll take it."

Jasten took a plate and sat against the wall. He ate methodically, without the vigor that Lila was displaying. Then again, he was suffering from heat sickness, not having just gone through a battle for his life. Still, I kept half an eye on him.

Maks and I took our plates and went to the window. "We can plan this way, it's the closest we're going to get to a map." He paused and picked up a piece of the bread. "Though I don't know how we are going to plan for something we can't see."

He wasn't wrong. I filled him in on what we'd seen from the vantage of the roof. "That main gate, it looks like it would be a straight shot all the way to the palace, but there's no way to get to it past the golems. Not without them hot on our asses. We can outrun them, but then we'd have golems at our back, and a dick of a demon at our front."

Jasten snorted. "A dick of a demon, yes . . ."

"There has to be a way, we'll figure it out," Maks said. "You always do." He bumped me gently with his hip and I leaned into him as I nodded.

"Good thing you have me." I made myself take the first bite, scooping up a huge bite of hummus and soft bread. I had to restrain myself from moaning. How long since we'd eaten fresh, soft bread? Once I got going on the food, I didn't slow until my belly was full. Which wasn't that much. My appetite had shrunk over the months of travel and little to no food on a regular basis.

"Please, pour me a drink," Lila said. "I want to sleep for a while. I want to just forget for a little while."

I put my own plate down and poured her a drink

into one of the cups, then poured for the rest of us. Jasten took the drink, sniffed it, and then snapped it back in a single gulp.

And promptly passed out.

I raised my eyebrows at Maks. "Lightweight over there."

On cue, Jasten began snoring, his head slumping to his chest. A slurping sound turned me around. Lila was face first into the tankard. I pulled her out again, but this time it was too late. She was singing under her breath.

"Oh, I miss Fen," she cried. Huge tears rolled down her face. "I didn't tell him how I felt! I was so busy being scared that he'd hurt me like that fuddermucker . . ." She was sobbing and I gathered her up in my arms and just held her as she cried herself to sleep between gulping sobs.

"Not so much for me," I said. I took a small sip of the țuică, enjoying the sweet plum alcohol as it slid down my throat and warmed my belly and the memories it brought with it. The first time Maks and I had kissed had been encouraged with this sweet drink.

Maks took my hand and led me to one of the beds.

There were no words as he sat first, then pulled me down into his arms as I held onto Lila. The three of us curled up together, and there in that rickety bed I felt as close to the family of my heart as I could be.

"We'll finish this, one way or another," Maks said. "Together."

I tightened my hold on him. "I won't leave you behind again. I promise."

"Better not," he grumbled and kissed the top of my head. I smiled and leaned my head against him, closing my eyes. No one had so much as taken off clothes, never mind weapons.

You never knew when you'd have to fight. And let's be honest, it was usually when you let your guard down that the bad guys showed up.

Which is why when the ruckus on the stairs started, waking me and Maks, I was not surprised at all.

I sat up and looked at the window. Dawn was not far off. Lila was snoring, and Jasten muttered in his sleep.

"No, no, no."

"Out the window with you two," Maks whispered. "I'll handle this."

I took Lila with me as I climbed out the window, tucking her inside my cloak as I went. I made my way up to the roof and ducked out of sight from the window.

The door banged open less than ten seconds later. "We's looking for three travelers, you them?"

The gruff voice was not real subtle.

"Just me and my sleeping friend over there, he had too much to drink. Again," Maks said, exasperation heavy in his voice.

"Huh. Two out of three. But no woman. Leave them

be. Guy said no woman came in last night here neither."

"We gotta be thorough though, boss said so. Said she was a tricky bitch. Said she could hide real good."

There was some scuffling. "Fine! Let me check out the window."

"Out the window?" Maks sounded incredulous, but I could hear the tension in his voice. "We are five stories up! I'd like to meet someone who could fly though, so yeah, check." Of course he couldn't put too much effort into trying to keep them from looking out the window.

I shifted to my house cat form in a flash. Just in case they decided to climb on out to find us, it was less likely they'd be bothered by a cat. And a small dragon?

Clinging to the roof and Lila at the same time was . . . not easy. She began to slip. I dug my claws into her sides, and she let out a yelp. "Bugger off!"

I bit down on her nose, clamping her mouth shut. So now I was totally tied up in keeping Lila from moving with my front end, my back end digging into the roof tiles the best I could. And I was slipping.

"What that noise?" the gruff voice shouted.

Fuck me. I couldn't let the now slightly squirming, grumbling Lila go. And I couldn't shift back to my human form as the head of the guard was just below us. I could see his light brown hair blowing in the wind.

With a quick yank I jerked us both backwards, over

the peak and down the other side of the crown, pulling Lila along with me into the hollow between two sections of the roof.

"Birds," the guard grumbled. "Damn birds."

I breathed a sigh of relief. My nose twitched at the smell of tobacco curling through the crisp night air. I released Lila and slowly turned to see someone sitting in the shadows. Only the tip of his pipe glowed red, other than that I couldn't see anything.

Which was saying something because I could see very well in the dark.

The sounds of the guards leaving tugged at my ears, but I didn't dare to take my eyes from the man on the roof.

"Clever trick," he whispered after a few minutes of silence.

I let out a low hiss. He'd seen me shift. Well, fuck it then. I shifted back to two legs and scooped Lila up. "I'd say thanks, but I don't think that would be wise of me." I kept my voice low, quiet.

"No?" He tipped his head, or at least the shadow of his head tipped to one side. "Why is that?'

The cold rolled off him, and I realized then that was what was giving the night the crisp feeling. Not the world around us, but *him*. The thing in front of me was not human, not shifter, nothing that I wanted to deal with and that made me want to hiss again, even though I was on two legs.

"Demon, right?"

His laughter was deep and the cold intensified around us. "You say that like you aren't quite sure."

"Close enough, I'm guessing," I said. I wasn't willing to take my eyes off him. "Pearso?"

His pipe flared a little, and for a moment I caught a glimpse of his features. "Oy-ya. What are you doing up here, cat?"

I kept Lila tucked close. "Avoiding problems."

"Or running toward them?" he offered.

"Both," I said, and he laughed again, softer this time.

"You going into the city? Trevalon is not for the faint of heart." He pointed with his pipe to the demon gates, his bony long fingers emerging for a split second from the shadows. "Asag is not going to make it easy on you to get to him. None of them are. You're just a game to the big man. A fun time. A way to pass the days."

None of them? Wait, what was he saying?

Just like the woman at the front of the city, I wondered if this one somehow recognized me.

I slid back a few feet, closer to the edge, not liking that the woman at the front might have been a demon too. "You got something you want to say, then say it."

The pipe flared bright, and his eyes picked up the red glow. "Oy-ya. We like our city, we don't like Asag, but he's what we's got. You threaten both if you plan to try and kill him. That's problematic. We all would come for you then."

Lilith shivered on my back, and her whisper was faint. *I could be the answer to their dark prayers. I could be their queen.*

I blew out a careful breath. "Who said anything about Asag?"

He tapped his pipe on the palm of his hand, dumping out the embers. The flesh didn't burn. It steamed. "Oy-ya. Some will help. Most will hurt. That's all I can say."

"Which are you?" I was right above the window now, feeling the edge with the heels of my boots.

Again, I couldn't see him smile, but I could feel it in his words. "Me? I'm Chaos. But my friends call me Pearso. You met my friend earlier."

What friend was he referring to? I grimaced. "Mate," I called down to Maks because I didn't want to use Maks's name. He stuck his head out and I glanced down quick enough that I could hand him Lila. I wanted to talk more with this demon named Chaos, but not if I had to defend myself and Lila too.

I looked back to where he'd been sitting in the shadows.

Just in that brief flash, the demon had disappeared. Damn it all to the center of the desert!

"What is it?" Maks asked.

"Wait, I'm taking a quick look for someone." I made myself reach for the sword strapped to my back even while Maks tried to get my attention. I reached for Lilith. I let my fingers brush against the handle, and she stirred in my mind.

What?

"Would other demons work for Asag, or be against him?" I stepped lightly across the roof, checking the shadows. Looking for the glowing pipe.

Depends. Her tone was sour. She was still pissed that I'd beaten her. To be fair, she hadn't really known what she was up against when she took me on for reals, thinking she'd get to run the show and use my body to do it.

I was a dirty fighter when it came to survival, demon or no demon.

The roof was large, but I went over it twice before I was satisfied that the shadowy figure of Chaos was gone. But where had he gone to? I'd heard nothing, smelled nothing except for his pipe. Even the scent that I'd started to associate with demons hadn't been there.

As far as I could tell there were no other open windows. I drew in a breath, looking for the scent of the pipe, but there was nothing now, it was completely gone. As if he had never sat here talking with me.

I went back to our side, dropped down and flipped through our room window.

"What was it?" Maks asked. "Did you see something?"

"I think another demon." I kept my voice low. Both Lila and Jasten had slept through the guards' visit.

Maks frowned. "*Another* demon?"

"Well, as opposed to Lilith or Asag. Or the stable boy. Or the woman at the front gates," I muttered.

Maks and I shared a long look. "You think everyone is a demon here?"

I gave a slow nod. "I'm pretty sure they knew we weren't, and that's why we're being bothered. They already know who we are. We don't fit."

Fuck, they—all the demons—knew. But did they know that we'd figured it out? That was harder to say.

I paced the room, tapping my fingers against my thighs. "He was smoking a pipe, but I couldn't see his face. He was all shadows and I should have been able to see him, but couldn't. He called himself Chaos, but Jasten called him Pearso earlier—"

"Chaos," Jasten said quietly. "That is . . . not good if he is identifying as Chaos."

I raised my eyebrows at Jasten who was suddenly awake. "You know something about that kind of demon?" How much had he heard? Had he been faking the sleeping?

Jasten's eyes were half-shuttered. "The demons that favor the shadows, they are trouble." He rubbed a hand across his chest and winced. "It tells me that Asag has pissed off a number of demons. There might be another going after the throne that he so covets."

"So we'd be trading one demon for another?" I snorted. "That's not ideal."

"While you may be loath to believe this, there are

worse demons than Asag who could have ruled here," Jasten said quietly. "I am *telling* you that there are far worse." His voice wavered and his eyes lifted to mine. The green was ringed thickly with black, and just a hint of red glimmer.

My eyebrows slowly climbed. "Who are you?"

His eyes shot to mine and there was a flicker in them as though the green would come back. "Why would you ask that?"

I launched myself at him, slamming him against the wall, running on an instinct that danger was here, right in the room with us. I pinned his throat with my forearm as I let a low growl trickle from my lips.

His eyes shifted fully from the green I'd known to a solid black that glowed with red lights, and his voice reverberated weirdly in his throat with a low bass and a high soprano at the same time. "Fairly played. Your friend was near death; we took his body for our own. We did not think you would notice. We have let him guide you thus far, using his memories. He is asleep, so it is a time for us to speak."

"You aren't very good at *not* being demon like," Maks said.

He'd suspected too. I reached back with my other hand to Lilith, just touching the handle, not actually gripping it.

"Who are you?"

I let my fingers hover over the handle of the sword, not quite touching.

59

"We saved you both," Jasten said in his weird voice. "Because we need Asag to be taken home, to the demon realm. The gates between the realms must be closed. This world is not ours the way he has tried to make it."

Bullshit! It is ours for the taking, we were always meant to be the masters and I want my fair share of it!

Lilith's rage rolled through me, but I tamped it down and took my hand away from the sword, though it felt like sticky sap tried to keep me holding onto it. The strange dark eyes locked on me, and then slowly slid so that they took in the sword handle no doubt peeking over my shoulder. "You still carry Lilith?"

"Does a dog carry fleas?" I muttered. "Of course I do! I can't put her down and risk what she would do to another." His words sunk into me. "Wait . . . you saved us?"

Jasten rolled his head side to side. "I am Nico and Soleil. We are . . . the ones tasked with bringing Asag home by our master. He is our responsibility."

I wondered at that. I mean, this was two demons infesting a person. A parasite. And they wanted us to trust them. A snort escaped me. "Look, I don't trust Lilith. I don't trust you—either of you. I don't trust that fellow Chaos up there. I have no doubt that you saved us for a reason that works in your favor—"

"The path must be opened to us, by *you* if we are to reach him," Jasten said, only this time his voice was a little more his own. Or at least, not the quavering of two voices trapped in one set of vocal cords.

I stared at him, Maks at my side. "Why?"

Jasten's eyes closed. "Because one of the rules is that you must be mortal to face him. So no demon could come at him. He was clever that way, setting up the rules. So very clever."

A chill rippled down my spine and a horrible, terrifying thought stole my breath. I stumbled back and into Maks. He grabbed hold of me. "What is it? Zam, what's wrong?"

All I could do was stare at Jasten. "The pathway is closed. No one can get to Asag right now?"

"Correct."

"And when I open it, others could use it." I whispered because I was afraid that I was right.

Jasten—Nico and Soleil—gave a slow nod. "Now you are beginning to see. The only way we can take him home is through you. But . . . the only way another demon could take his place, is also through you the second you defeat him. The timing will be . . . tricky."

Which explained why the shadow demon on the roof had not done more than interact carefully with me. "They're all waiting—the other demons. And then it will be a race at the end, they will gather around while you fight your final battle with him. That's what you're telling me?"

Seriously, every time I thought I had a handle on

what was happening, this kind of shit came up. And it stole my breath away with the horror of it.

Maks kept a gentle hold on me. "Then there is a way around it. There must be. These demon rules will have a loophole. They're demons, after all."

Jasten lifted both hands above his head, palms to the sky. "Perhaps, but none that we have seen. And Soleil can see somewhat ahead to the future." His eyes rolled and turned a pale blue. This was Soleil?

The voice was more soprano now. Feminine like before. "The main gates must be opened. To succeed with *your* task, I see that clearly. The gates . . . must open."

"The main gates," I said. "The ones with the magic on them, and the golems guarding them?"

Jasten—or maybe Soleil—nodded. "Correct."

It felt like she wanted to say more, her mouth opening, shutting, and then she shook her head.

The silence in the room was heavy. Thick like mud wrapping itself around my legs and sucking me under. This was a death trap that we faced. "If another demon takes his place—"

Jasten snapped fingers on both hands. "Asag is a child in our world, despite his age here. The demon who would take him out would indeed be a monster that would ravage the land. You do not want this."

"Why would you care about that?" Maks asked. "What does it matter to you whether our land is safe or not?"

"While we don't care one way or another what happens here, our task is one that we must complete, or we too will be . . . ended." Jasten shrugged.

"Self-preservation," Maks said.

From my back, Lilith chuckled, the sound bouncing against the walls, over and over. Lila rolled over in the bed where Maks had put her, whimpering.

"Shut that thing up," she grumbled, lashing her tail back and forth like a pissed off cat.

Good thing you were stronger than me, purred Lilith. *Or I would take you straight to Asag and then take the throne.*

I wasn't sure that anyone else heard her, but I felt the implications. That she had let me win, knowing that if she'd inhabited my body, she never would have made it to her brother. I didn't think that was the case at all. She had fought for all she was worth and lost.

I blinked and looked back at Maks. "This is a fucking mess if I ever saw one."

"One thing at a time," he said. "Let's get to Reyhan and Fen, then free the dragons. Free the golden dragon and find a way to open the main gate. Then we can deal with Asag and the other demons."

He said it as if any of that was simple. Just steps in a plan that were straightforward.

I nodded out of reflex, but Jasten was shaking his head. And I hated that I was in agreement with the pair of demons. Because if we didn't think about what was coming, we couldn't be ready for it.

"You are thinking too linear. The path is not linear. None of it is. When dealing in demons, you must be ready for anything and everything to change," Jasten grumbled.

"What we need is someone who has banished demons before." I rubbed my hands over my face, then looked to my mate.

Maks paled. "I think . . . I think I can help with that."

FIVE

"What do you mean? Does the knowledge in your head from the Jinn masters tell you something about banishing demons?" I turned fully to Maks, putting my back to Jasten. Not that I trusted the demons in him—not a chance. But I did believe that they wanted and needed me alive. At least for the time being, and that meant that in the moment, they could be trusted.

Sort of.

Maks ran a hand through his hair and leaned his hip against the edge of the only table in the room. "There was a spirit that reached out to me after you and I were separated. I thought he was my father. He presented himself as Marsum. Knew things that Marsum had known, but then, there was more. He knew things about the Beast from the East, about what I was facing that I felt Marsum would not have in his head. Marsum and the other Jinn masters had a big blank for what was over this way." He looked at me, his blue eyes full of concern. "When I finally called him out, he admitted that he was a demon hunter. And that I was from his bloodline. That was how he connected with me."

Jasten let out a low grumble. "I knew it, that meddling Jinn could not leave well enough alone!"

The pieces were slowly coming together. "Male Jinn were demon hunters here? That's why they were all killed off?"

"By the sounds of it," Maks said. "Explains why they were hunted out of existence. Or near enough. And why Vahab was stuffed into a box."

"Vase," Lila mumbled in her semi-sleep state. "He was in a lady's vase."

Maks began to slowly pace the room. "I could try to connect with Roshawn. See if he is still hanging around."

"He most likely is," Jasten said with his dual voice again. I cringed.

"Could you stop doing that? One or the other; the double voice shit is grating," I snapped.

Jasten did a sharp blink and cleared his throat, his eyes solid black again. A whisper of something leaving Jasten's body and he straightened up more. "Is this better?"

I nodded and pointed a finger at Jasten. "What do you know about Roshawn?"

"He . . . worked with Vahab, Mamitu and Pazuzu to try and stop Asag. They nearly did it. Nearly." Jasten shifted his weight a little on the bed and closed his eyes. "This man is dying. We can only keep him alive for a short while. So you must decide quickly what you will do next."

My jaw ticked but I didn't dare even reach for Jasten's hand. Not with him hosting two demons. "Keep him alive."

"We are. He was holding death's hand when we found him. He wants to help you, he wants to help his daughter," Jasten said. "Soleil has left his body so that there is less strain, but even that will not fully keep him alive."

It was my turn to close my eyes. I was not close with Jasten, I doubted Maks would consider himself close with the shifter, but Reyhan . . . I was almost certain this was her father. Even though he denied it, I knew it was just Nico and Soleil covering their asses. "When are demons less likely to be active? Or is there a time?" I asked.

"Pre-dawn, that is the best time to try to slip by unnoticed," Jasten said.

I gave him a quick nod. "Then we sleep for three hours. We go before dawn, and you two will lead the way. We cannot get in through the main gates, not with the golems there."

Jasten closed his eyes. "As you wish. There is another path. Though you may find it unpleasant."

I didn't want to point out that saying it was unpleasant was likely an understatement. We were sneaking into a demon city full of unknowns.

"I eat unpleasant for breakfast," Lila grumbled.

I moved to the bed Lila was in and scooped her up, holding her tight to my chest. Maks double checked the door and tucked a chair under the handle for added measure against another raid.

"Sleep while you can," I said. "We will need all the rest we can get."

Curled up with him and Lila, I let myself fall under the spell of sleep.

THREE HOURS PASSED IN A BLINK, and I fought awake, jerking up to a sitting position as though something had startled me. A soft scuffle at the window spun me around. But it was only Lila, sitting on the edge, staring out at the palace. The fog. And ultimately toward Fen and Reyhan.

"We have to go," she said softly. "Fen is hiding his fear as best he can. But I can feel it now."

I reached for her, and as I did, I mentally reached for the connection to Reyhan. She was scared, but not terrified. There was a bud of hope inside of her, and I fed it with a little of my energy. The less afraid she was, the better. Fen's connection was not as strong, but it was also there. He was not terrified either, but Lila was right, there was fear and worry aplenty.

That was good. Or at least I was hoping it was good. Neither of them were injured.

Maks rolled out of bed, and we had our bags tossed over his shoulders. Jasten was the last of us to get up, his joints creaking as though he were a far older man than his face said.

I let myself really look at him. At the edges of his bones under his skin, the dark circles below his eyes, the tremble in his hands, the overall fragility of his movements. He was not the strong, healthy shifter I'd met before. "You being inside of him. Is that killing him too?"

"Yes." He nodded slowly. "But he would have died had we not taken his body. It is what the humans call—"

"Catch-22," Lila muttered as she wrapped herself around my neck. I pulled my hood up.

I stared at Jasten. "Does he know that we are going to save his daughter? That alone will give him strength." Family bonds were everything in a shifter's world. Most especially those between parents and children.

Jasten nodded. "He knows. And he knows we are helping."

"You think we can use the stairs this time?" Lila asked quietly, her tail lashing. She was trying to stay cool, but the tension was rolling off her. She wanted to move.

Maks motioned for quiet as he put his ear to the

door. "Two guards outside. I can hear them breathing. But why? Why at our door?"

That was my question too. "No one saw us all come in," I said softly. "But if we're right, and they all know that we aren't demons like them . . ."

Jasten swayed a little. "I'd lay money on Chaos. The one you spoke with likely tipped them off. He thrives on pandemonium. This would make things interesting. The guards will not let any of us pass. And if they take a close look at me they will see what resides within this body."

Lila grumbled but peeled herself off my neck. "Let's go then."

I put a hand on Maks and lowered my voice. "We'll take the rooftop out, that's doable."

He looked at the door. "Good idea. That will cover our tracks far better, maybe it even buys us more time. If we're lucky." Maks pointed at the table, and together we lifted it, setting it against the door, grimacing as it groaned. The longer it took the guards to come in once they decided to try, the better.

Lila led the way, flying out the window and up to the roof. Maks shifted to his caracal form, and followed her with a bounce, black-tipped ears swiveling about as he listened for danger.

"You next," I said to Jasten. He'd be the biggest of us as a jungle cat. He blew out a breath.

"I do not know if this body has the strength for it. This body is weak."

I grimaced and reached out for his hand—sure, Asag had stolen all our magic. But he couldn't steal my alpha abilities. That wasn't magic. That was just who I was to the core of my bones. Jasten took my hand, a curious look on his face until I pushed some of my energy into him. He wasn't technically family, but in a roundabout way I could consider him such. Reyhan was family, so her father was too by association. Even if he was infested with a demon at the moment.

He gasped and color flooded his face as some of my energy slid into him, stealing away the ashen gray tones and stilling the tremble in his arms. Before he could speak, I said one word, pushing my power into it. I could feel the drag on my own reserves, but I had to do this. We needed a guide to get to Asag, and this was all we had.

A half dead shifter full of a demon that we couldn't trust.

"Shift."

His body slid from two legs to four and he stumbled a little, his balance off. "Now, out the window." I didn't have time for lollygagging.

He did as he was told, flowing out through the space, gone like a shadow in the night with a flick of his tail.

I stepped through the doorway in my mind, took on my small house cat shape, and struggled for a moment to get my bearings. The door behind me rattled ever so slightly. "Room check, open the fuck up."

Yup, time to go. Taking a quick breath, I bounded out the window and up to the roof where my friends were waiting. Leaning over the ledge of the roof, I batted the edge of the window until it was shut. Let them figure that out.

The four of us moved through the night, silent, stealthy as the thumps below us told us that the guards were tearing the room apart. All quiet . . . except for Lila.

She was looking back over her shoulder, toward the palace, and ran straight into a metal stove pipe. She clanked it hard enough that the thing clanged like a damn gong reverberating through the air.

Voices called up from all over the top floor. "What's going on up there? Beggars! They took to the roof!"

"Sorry!" she whispered. "I was thinking about Fen!"

"Hurry." I kept my voice low. "Straight to the stable, fast as you can."

We raced across the roof, leapt to the next rooftop lower than us, then again and again until we were stepping up to the back door of the stable, the smell of hay and horses filling my nose.

With one exception. There was a tang of metal on the night air too. And the smell of demons was everywhere.

More guards. One on either side at the back of the

stable told me there would be more at the front as the wind spun and brought me their scents.

Fuck.

"Let me go first, I'll take a gallop out and lead them away," I said, already dreading another shift between forms. I'd not been this tired in a long time. "Meet me at the main gate, I'll circle back."

Jasten shook his head, ears flopping a little. "That main gate is not the best way in—Asag will expect you to try and sneak through the fog when it's thickest right before dawn, never mind the golems. Not to mention that the other demons will be on your path in a flash. Leave the horses. Follow me. This is where we can help."

I did not want to leave Balder and Dancer. I looked to Maks and his eyes narrowed. He wasn't sure either. The hornless unicorns were faster than anything else on land, with the exception of perhaps another unicorn.

But if we were going to let the demon inside Jasten lead, then this was the moment. This was the chance we had to make it happen.

I gave him a slow nod. "Go."

Jasten spun and leapt away from the stable, using the shadows of the buildings around us to cover his bigger body. Lila ran alongside me, her wings brushing my back.

Jasten led us not toward the castle gates. But south, deeper into the city outskirts.

I wasn't getting a bad feeling, at least not until he slid to a stop in front of a broken-down building that had scorch marks all over the timbers. It had been burned out sometime recently, as the scent of char was heavy even in the still pre-dawn air.

He slid through a small opening that had been left after a number of timbers had fallen down, criss-crossing one another. Maks bounced through after him and Lila and I followed.

The hair along my back stood up in a straight puff as my feet landed inside the building itself.

"Jasten."

"Here. We must do this quickly. There are wardings all over this place. It won't be long before they are on us."

His body stumbled back to two feet, and he swayed and went to his knees. "I need hands to open this. Help me."

I stepped through that doorway in my mind and damn if I didn't wobble again, my knees shaking until I locked them hard for the second time in less than an hour. Too many times back and forth from two to four legs in a short space, and then giving Jasten my energy had drained me down more than I realized.

Maks was beside me in a flash, helping me stand, his hands under my elbows, steadying me. "Lila, keep watch out one of the top windows, watch the street," he said.

I nodded. It was a good idea to keep watch of who was following. Or if we'd made a clean break of it.

Lila shot up through the burnt rafters and snugged in against one of the window casings. "I've got eyes on the street, no one yet." Her voice drifted down to us. It's hard to yell and whisper at the same time, but she managed.

Maks and I made our way over to Jasten who was carefully picking up some of the downed wood, dragging it aside. "Under here."

I grabbed the end of a timber and lifted, using my legs and arms in tandem to get it a few feet off the ground. Before I could even say his name, Maks was there, sliding his hands around the large timber.

He helped me, taking some of the weight, and we rotated it off to the side which freed up a number of the smaller timbers that we could each move individually.

"Hurry," Jasten whispered. "This body . . . is nearly done."

Lowering it to the ground carefully, I winced as it squeaked, rubbing up against another part of the interior.

"Here, here," Jasten said. "Do you see this symbol?"

I looked down at the floorboards. "The crescent moon."

"That is his symbol. There will be markers along the way. Follow them." He bent and pried up a board. Just one board. There was no simple trapdoor in the floor. This was basically a dug hole, with very little room.

"Best if we were smaller," I said softly.

Damn it, another shift. Already I could feel my need to sleep off the back and forth dragging at me. A quick look at Maks and I could see that he wasn't far behind me. His shifting seemed to cost him more, so fewer times back and forth bottomed him out.

"We have to," he said softly, echoing my unspoken thoughts. That hole was small enough for a child to crawl through, not an adult.

"Guys," Lila whisper-yelled. "We've got company."

She flew down, grabbing at my shoulder and dragging me toward the hole. "Lila, what is after us?"

Her eyes were wide. "Dragon."

CHAPTER
SIX

Dragon. Lila's one-word warning was all it took to get us moving.

"Fire breathers?" I took a look at the scorch marks on the building as I tried to pull out what Jasten—or more truly, what the demon—had given me. "Ah, fuck."

"Go, go!" Jasten growled. "We will find you. It will be another body, but we will find you as soon as we can."

I shifted at the same time as Maks and we leapt down into the hole in the ground, Lila right with us, tumbling hard into us. The hole was straight down at least fifteen feet.

The three of us hit the bottom, knocking the wind out of me at least.

"Run," Jasten snarled down to us, and then he dropped the cover over the hole.

I didn't wait to ask him what was happening up there, I had a pretty good suspicion why he was telling us to run. I squinted my eyes in the dim light and raced forward, Maks right behind me, Lila behind him.

"They're going to firebomb the place," Lila yelped. "I saw the dragon prepping, and that flame is going to come straight down here. It will seek us out!"

A boom from behind us, the crackling of distant flames and a sudden burst of heat spoke volumes.

Not that I hadn't believed her, but for a moment I'd hoped she was wrong. Already the light in the tunnel brightened as the fire shot toward us. The upside was, it allowed us to see where we were going.

The downside . . . it was heating up fast, eating up all the air.

Fear tangled up in my throat, because there were no offshoots, no paths that were offered other than the one we were on, so if there was a dead end, we were dead. The demons could have been conning us all along.

Fucking demons. I'd come back from the grave and haunt them if they had tricked us.

Lila yelped but I couldn't look back. "Lila!"

"I'm okay, just go!" she screeched.

The heat was increasing rapidly, stealing the air around us, and that's when I realized that we had a secondary problem.

No air.

No breathing.

No fuel for running.

My muscles spasmed as I tried to suck a breath that wasn't there.

Feet stumbling, I managed a few more inches before I fell on my face. *I'm going to die in a dark hole like a rat*, was my thought. Which was morbidly amusing considering my feline nature. I'd have laughed if I had any energy or wind to do so.

Laying there, I reached a paw back for Maks, found him. Then Lila crawled up and over us both. "Flames gone. Give air minute."

I closed my eyes, counted to twenty and then sucked in a deep breath. The air was warm, but the oxygen was back.

I took a few more drags before I pushed to my feet. "Maks?"

"Five more minutes," he grumbled into the dirt. I pushed his face to the side so he wasn't face down as before.

"Come on, Toad." Lila plucked at one of the black hairs from his ears and he grumped fully awake. "Don't dawdle."

Trembling, he got to his feet and the three of us slowly padded through the now pitch-dark tunnel. "Was this a trap that didn't quite catch us?" Lila asked quietly. "It feels like we got away, but maybe like they let us?"

Yup, that was the question I was asking myself too. But my gut said otherwise. "No, I don't think so. It doesn't make sense to kill us, not if the other demons need us to get to Asag first." That being said, we'd be sitting ducks the minute we opened up that path.

"Maybe you're just too exhausted to care anymore," Lila said. The swish of her wings and tail were the only sounds in the tunnel. Maks and I were silent on our padded feet.

"Could be," I murmured. "Or could be that Nico and Soleil really want to take Asag home."

Home.

I frowned. "Lilith, what kind of connection does Asag have Nico and Soleil?" I knew that she was his sister, she'd let that slip out.

Nico whelped him.

My brain stuttered a minute. Whelped. "Nico is his parent? Your father? Why didn't they want to save you? What about Soleil?" Where did the beautiful demon fit into this?

Maks sucked in a sharp breath. Lila let out a slow hiss. "Well, that's messy."

Messy indeed.

Lilith went quiet after that. She wanted to take Asag's throne, wanted to kill him for confining her to a weapon. Nico and Soleil wanted to take him 'home' and close the opening between demons and this world. They'd said nothing about Lilith.

"I'm going to take it you have issues with your dad and stepmom?" I offered. "Bad daughter, huh? Black sheep and all that shit?"

Still silence. Fine. It didn't really matter anyway. We had to manage with the hands we were dealt, and this was ours.

"Light ahead," Lila said.

She was right, the darkness was not so complete now. That little bit of illumination allowed me to see the tunnel around us. The scratch marks. The bits of scales.

"This was how Castor escaped," I said softly. Castor had been lost in the desert when we'd come across him. A friend to Lila for a little while, but too scared to be a match for her. "This is the escape tunnel he used. It has to be."

And if one had escaped through this route, there was a chance that there would be guards to keep anyone else from escaping again. But then, why wouldn't they have covered the escape route?

To trap those who might try again? Yeah, that was my thought too. Demons were tricky fuckers.

I grabbed Lila's tail as she went to step out, not into sunshine, but into a thick, nearly glowing fog. It was still night, but the fog was reflecting light, giving off a strange shimmer.

She looked back at me, and I shook my head. Wait. We needed to wait a moment. Rushing now and getting our heads cut off was a terrible idea.

I crept past her on my belly and put just my nose to the edge of the tunnel and drew in a deep, slow breath.

That same smell of iron and copper weapons

curled through me. A hint of leather. The smell of demons. My ears swiveled. The creak of leather and the shuffle of boots on the sand as weight was shifted from one leg to the other.

At least two demon guards. I backed up and, using a claw, scratched three lines in the dirt going in different directions. Maks and Lila both nodded. We would have a better chance if we ran in different directions into the fog. Better yet . . . I pointed a claw tip at my chest, then motioned for them to wait.

Lila was already shaking her head. I dragged her backward, deeper into the tunnel.

"They will not be looking for a cat," I whispered. "They *will* be looking for a dragon. You are part of what they want, remember?"

Maks tucked himself in next to me and Lila.

"You are going to lead them away?" he asked.

"You are from a demon hunter," I said. "You think they won't recognize a Jinn? Even like this?" I butted my nose against his. "And they are looking to keep the dragons in, not cats out."

"Point taken," he said softly. "So, you'll draw them off and then what? We don't know where we are going."

"I'll find you," I said. "I'll loop back around. If we're separated beyond this, head north toward the castle."

The theory and the plan were good, solid even. I liked it. I wasn't sure anyone else did. But they both knew as I did, that the plan was the best we were going to get under the circumstances. Not like we had anyone on the outside to distract them.

The three of us crept back to the mouth of the tunnel as one of the guards stuck his head down to peek in. "I'm sure I heard something—Aaaahhhh!"

I saw his face and I knew I couldn't wait. I shot out of the tunnel at him, hissing and scratching at his face. Forgetting that I had Lilith connected to me. Forgetting the damage that my claws would do when I had a powerful weapon blended into my very body and bones.

I cut his damn nose right off with a single swipe. Blood sprayed outward in an arc as he wheeled back and away, screaming. I took off with a burst of speed, running through the strange, heavy fog, feeling the moisture sinking into my fur.

There was the clatter of a spear thrown at me, and I ducked, flattening myself to the ground even as I zigged sideways. The spear missed, shooting off to the right. There was no way they'd think I was a regular cat now—not when I'd sliced the one guard's nose off. I wanted to sigh, but I had to keep moving and that meant I had no breath for sighing. The fog shifted and it reminded me of the deep fog in the desert before the lizard men had attacked us what seemed like a lifetime ago. When all we had to worry about was the Emperor. Funny how he seemed an easy opponent now.

I found a long brick wall and I pinned myself against it, hugging the shadows as I slowed my breathing. There was no sign of chase. No more spears clattering against the bricks around me.

Which was good and not good. There *was* the sound of pattering feet and then Lila burst out of the fog and slammed into me. I grabbed hold of her as we tumbled over one another. "Where is Maks?" I asked before we were even stopped rolling.

"He went to the left, I followed you. The two guards are freaking out. You slashed him up bad!" Lila whispered.

"I know! I didn't think about the damage Lilith would do." I blew out a breath and shook my head. "Let's go find Maks."

Which in the fog was not as easy as it might sound —not only were the sounds dampened, but the scents too.

The reverberating screams of 'fucking cat' could be heard bouncing around. It made our movements slow, trying to avoid the soldiers.

Not soldiers, you dumbass . . . lower level demons. Lilith's voice rumbled through me and I sucked in a breath. Great. Just great. I'd hoped that what I was smelling was not right.

"You think Nico and Soleil helped others escape this place? How else could they have known where the entrance was?" Lila asked quietly.

That was a good question. But who'd ever heard of a demon who was merciful, or kind for that matter? Or was it part of a bigger game to them? That I'd believe.

"Maybe. But it will be because it helped them somehow. Same reason they've been *helping* us. They need us. Maybe not even for the reasons they're saying."

We slunk around the edge of the brick wall. Was there ever going to be an opening? Even as I thought it, I searched the wall and found a small break, an opening just big enough for a not very big cat. One that had caracal fur on either side of it, torn out as Maks had shot through. I slipped through, and Lila followed.

"Jasten never would have made it this far," Lila said. "Is that why they just sent us through?"

"His body was dying, they didn't have long with him." That tugged at my heart strings. One day I'd tell Reyhan the story of her father. Of how he took on demons to help me get to her. Of how he sacrificed himself.

"That or again, it was part of a game we don't understand." I put my nose to the ground, picking up Maks's scent. To be sure I was on the right track, I reached out for the bindings that tied us together. He wasn't far at all. I picked up speed, leaping in his direction.

Maks had found another crevice to tuck himself into, waiting with nothing but a bit of whiskers visible.

"Maks?" I whispered to him.

He popped his head out. "That worked better than I thought it would."

I hurried over to him and bunted my head against his. "Let's go."

"Stay like this?" he asked.

"Seems to be working so far," I murmured. "We haven't set off any alarms."

That's what you think. Lilith snickered. *Fools. You sliced his nose off! The demons know you are here, which means Asag knows you are here.*

I took a better look around at what we were dealing with. "We don't have a map, and we need to get our bearings." I looked up at the top of the wall we were tucked next to. Before I could think better of it, I leapt up the brick wall, pulling myself to the top, claws digging through the mortar easily. Sitting there, I could see out across the sea of fog and the tips of the houses that were showing here and there.

Maks and Lila scrambled up to sit next to me. "Not a great view," Lila said.

"No, not really," I said.

From where we were, there were a few alley ways with walls, like what we were sitting on, set between buildings.

The sheer amount of buildings was good and bad. Lots of places to hide. But lots of places to have enemies hide too. Even as I thought it, shadows flowed between buildings—shadows that had the shape of tall, lanky men.

Yeah, that was not going to bode well. Shadows didn't move independently unless there was something seriously wrong.

Steeling myself, I reached for Lilith, tugging her out

of the depths of my mind. "Lilith, what kind of demons are we dealing with? Cause if you want a shot at your brother, we have to get through this city." Which meant it was in her best interest to help us.

Let me see.

Her words made me cringe. I let her climb further through my body until I felt her settle in my head. I blinked my eyes and it was like two images were superimposed on one another.

The shadows that I saw.

The demons that Lilith recognized.

"Those shadows you see, they are demons. *Instabilismori.*" I spoke but my voice was odd, warbling the way Jasten's had been. "A form of shapeshifting demon. They will form to your fears, and that is what you will face. You can banish them by throwing holy salt on them. Or you could use me, if you were brave enough."

I swallowed hard and pushed Lilith away. I had to close my eyes to do it as she clung to her position where she could see out my eyes. But I didn't dare leave her that close to the surface.

"Enough," I growled and used my alpha strength to put her down.

Her laughter rolled to my lips and I clamped it back as she settled somewhere near my left big toe. At least that's what it felt like.

"You okay?" Maks leaned into me, giving me his strength without being asked.

I nodded and leaned back into him. "Where the hell do we find holy salt?" Because there was no way I'd use Lilith until there was no other choice. Pushing her down had been too difficult, especially with all the shifts I'd been making, taking my energy down each time.

"Could she be lying?" Maks asked. As we watched, shadows flickered again. Were they closer?

"Yes, she could be. But I don't think so. Let's be honest, there won't be holy salt anywhere within a hundred miles of this place. Not if Asag has anything to say about it. And she wants me to use her."

Yeah, those shadows *were* closer. The light around us dimmed suddenly and I looked up. "Where did the sun go?"

It was early morning. They sun should have been shining brightly, burning off the fog.

Demons like the dark. They're stronger in it, Lilith said, derision thick in her voice. *If you can't find holy salt, and you won't use me, then something bright that throws a lot of light will work on these.*

I relayed that bit of information to Lila and Maks. Lila snorted. "I don't know which would be harder to find. But we'd better do something soon, or we're going to get overrun by shadows. Think we can just sneak past them?"

Before I could answer, one of the dragons let out a low moaning growl that I felt all the way down my spine to the tip of my tail. I couldn't help the way my fur stood up along my back in response to the guttural resonance. As if on cue, more of the dragons called out, mournful cries that shattered the stillness of the air.

"We need to set them free," Lila said, her claws digging into the brick wall.

"And if we do that, the demons will be able to follow us easily," Maks said. "They are the bait, Lila. They are the trap that Asag knows we would walk into."

Her frustrated growl turned into a rumbling hiss. "I hate him, I will tear his damn balls off and spit acid in his eyes!"

I like her.

I ignored Lilith.

"Why don't they break out?" I wondered out loud.

"They are younger dragons for the most part. These would be only a few years old. Barely teenagers by our standards," Lila answered, her voice laced with pain. "And if he's keeping them weak somehow, then they won't have any energy to break free."

Broken children, with no parent to guide them, caged by a demon to steal their power. Even as we sat there, the sky above us crackled with a stark blue lightning. I crouched, Maks and Lila mimicking me, flattening to the top of the wall.

The bars on the cages suddenly began to glow with a brilliant blue light that matched the lightning, and the dragons inside howled and threw themselves around their enclosures. Their screams slammed against my ears, burrowing into my skull with the force of a thousand arrows. I grabbed at Lila feeling her muscles bunch as if she would fly to save them.

She couldn't save them. Not yet. Not here.

Maks helped and we pinned her down as she howled with them, her voice caught up with all of theirs, screaming in pain and begging for release. There were no words, and yet we heard them clearly.

Save us.

A choir of pain and sorrow, of fury and a savage need to fight back whipped through the fog and the dark sky. "Lila, we will get them out." I spoke right in her ear. "We will, I promise you that. We will free them all."

Her howls turned into sobs, and I just clung to her, and Maks to both of us as the blue lights in the cages faded and with it, the sounds of the dragons. Now I knew why they lay so still, so quiet.

There was no energy left over to allow them to do more than raise their heads—that blue light did, it drew off their power, their magic.

Letting them go one by one was not a possibility. We'd get caught—that was the bait that Asag had set out for us. The dragons would get caught with them having their energy and power stripped from them.

Yes, I was sure that was what we'd just seen—Asag draining them, prepping to face us. I clung to Lila as I spoke, feeling her sobs lessen with each passing moment.

"We have to get by them, we have to get to Asag and to the golden dragon. That's how we save them. The quicker the better," I said. But even as I spoke, I wondered just how we were going to do it. The palace was leagues away; on foot it would take days to get all the way there. Days to get through a city infested with demons and goddess only knew what else.

"How often do you think he takes their power?" Maks said softly.

I shook my head. "We'll count the time between now and the next. It could be days; it could be hours."

Lila shuddered and finally lifted her head. "So much pain, I felt it all the way through me."

"You're connected to them," I said. "The way you are connected to me and our family."

I didn't want to tell her that I'd felt it too, and by the look in Maks's eyes, he'd felt it as well.

She slowly nodded. "I am . . ."

I wondered if she could say it yet. That she was their queen and that was why she could feel everything so deeply. She shook her head. "They won't give us away, not the ones in the cages. But there could be others. Others that they use for hunting any who might try to get through the city."

That was what I was concerned about—more than Lila's ability to claim her spot amongst her own. Because we'd faced dragons before. And I wasn't real keen on doing it again.

SEVEN

The three of us crept as fast as we could along the top of the wall, until we could go no further without diving into the deep end of the demon city of Trevalon. I leapt down first, landing on the soft, loose ground. Sand. Lots of sand. From what we could see there were buildings, but I wasn't sure if there was anyone in them.

Strike that. We knew there were demons in them, only we didn't know just how many.

We trotted along, heading north, our footsteps making little noise on the loose sand. The first hour ticked by with nothing springing out at us, no battles, no shrieking monsters, yet I could feel the pressure in the air changing.

I could *feel* the weight of eyes on us from every open window and cracked door that we passed, growing heavier with every moment.

"This is bullshit," Lila whispered. "They're stalking us. But they aren't coming out, why?"

"Keep moving, stay quiet," I whispered. Maks led the way, Lila was in the middle and I was bringing up the rear. Another hour ticked by. Maybe we'd be okay, maybe they wanted us to get through to Asag?

Yeah, I didn't think so either. At least not all of them, if what the demon Pearso said was even a little bit true.

The silence was broken only by the scuffle of sand under our feet. I strained my ears and I was sure I was hearing things.

Because that sudden chirp . . . couldn't be what I thought I'd heard. The second one I was sure of my ears, and the sound had my heart in my throat. Rabisu. Fuck me with a prickle bush, you have got to be kidding me.

I herded Maks and Lila, dragging them back to the cover of a doorway that sat in the shadows. Lila knew that noise and was trembling already, her eyes wide as they could go. Maks had not had the pleasure of dealing with Rabisu.

I put a paw over his mouth, and he gave a quick nod and pinned himself flat, big ears swiveling.

Rabisu, how was I not surprised? Had they been brought here?

The Instabilismori you idiot. I told you they can be anything. They can even draw from your own mind, and

93

present as the thing that you fear the most. Her Irritation was thick.

"Right, don't have to be an asswipe about it," I whispered. Again, I relayed the information she gave me to Maks and Lila.

"Rabisu but not?" Lila kept her voice low. "I can almost get on board with that."

I motioned for her to be quiet as the chirping around us grew louder, more and more chiming in. We couldn't assume that the rabisu here would have the same weaknesses as those we'd dealt with in the jungle. Not for a second.

I mean, shit, they were demon rabisu.

A voice boomed through the air, silencing the chirps. A voice that I knew and hated.

Asag, the fucking Beast from the East.

"I know you are out there, Zamira. You must make it to me, still. How will you get past your old friends, the rabisu without their master? Without the unicorns? Without a jungle to hide in?" He laughed at that.

Of course, he was trying to goad me into speaking. I was not as stupid as he seemed to think. I rolled my eyes and Lila grimaced and nodded. Asag was a fucking tool.

His laughter faded. "You won't speak to me?"

The three of us didn't so much as squeak out a fart.

All around us, the air tensed, as if a giant hand were pressing down on us from above. We flattened ourselves to the old, desiccated floorboards, breathing in the dust. Praying that we didn't sneeze.

A rumble of thunder and Asag's voice rolled with it.

"I have your little friends here. Since you won't speak with me, perhaps I should just kill them?"

My jaw ticked. Speaking would only out us. And if we were dead, there would be no chance for Reyhan and Fen.

The pressure in the air increased and I couldn't help that my body fluffed up in response, hair standing on end right to the tip of my tail.

"Fine, if you wish to play the game like that. Then you have twenty-four hours to reach me before I kill them both. Good luck, bad luck cat."

The silence that fell after that was deafening.

Because the timing was impossible.

Even if we ran the entire distance, there was no way we could make it in twenty-four hours. Never mind the rabisu and whatever the fuck else he had planned up his sleeve with his demons that would slow us down along the way. With Balder and Dancer, we could have hopped on that straight path from the main gate and ridden hard, reaching the castle in under that twenty-four-hour time limit. Probably we could do it in twelve hours.

But we didn't have the horses, and the main roadway would leave us completely exposed.

Lila shot me a panicked look and I shook my head. Speaking would not help anything.

There was a particularly loud chirp, and a rabisu stepped into view, swinging its head this way and that as it sought us out. It was a demon so we couldn't kill it. We didn't have holy salt or brilliant light on us. And fighting with it would only pinpoint us for the others. And I had no doubt that there were other demons just waiting on us.

I looked around. The building we were pressed up against was wooden. We could go to the roof again. But that felt like something Asag wanted us to do, and after the pressure in the air above us, I had no doubt that he wanted that. We would be far more easily seen when we stepped out of the fog and up onto the rooftops. I slunk out of the shadows, placing each paw carefully, slowly, as the chirping faded behind us, the fake rabisu going the wrong way. A real rabisu would have been on us like a fat kid on a bag of sweets. There were other chirps but they were spread out in all directions, and none closer than that first one.

Score one for a demon pretending to be a rabisu.

I hunched my shoulders and kept moving, carefully placing each foot to remain as silent as possible. Until something under my left front paw tickled my toe beans.

The sand shifted under my feet, and I paused in my steps, heart in my throat once more. I flexed my paws so that my claws clung to what I stood on, because it was not solid ground. Where my feet rested, the sand filtered away, faster and faster, sliding and hissing as it fell into a massive pit below me. A pit full of writhing sand snakes, their eyes turning toward me, along with open mouths.

Lila squeaked and the chirping behind us picked up.

Sand snakes below. Rabisu all around us.

I was balanced on a thin rod that would have fallen if I'd been so much as an ounce heavier.

Maks and Lila went to either side of the pit, Maks's eyes narrowed as he inspected the edges. Lila's mouth hung open with horrow as she mouthed, *What now?*

Yeah, that was the question. What the fuck did I do now?

If I pushed off would the rods flex? Most likely. Which meant I'd just back up, take the edges and then . . .

A chirp behind us stopped me from even taking one step back, and I grimaced.

Which meant I had to tightrope walk my way off.

"Fuck." I only mouthed the word. I didn't say it out loud.

And yet . . . the rabisu chirped again, its feet kicking sand toward me as it hurried. I took one step and the thin wooden rods vibrated under my foot.

The sand snakes below hissed, sliding over one another to get closer. I glanced down only to see the glimmer of red in their eyes. Demons or at the very least demon made. Great.

"Screw this," Lila growled and leapt into the air,

swooped over me and scooped me up as the rods fell away and the rabisu lunged for us. We spun a little and she landed us next to Maks right up against the buildings. I whistled at the rabisu and it ran toward us, fingers and arms outstretched.

The rabisu didn't look down. It fell into the pit of sand snakes. For a split second it was not the faceless rabisu, but something else.

A dark shadow with burning yellow-orange eyes. The shadow fell though, that was the only good thing.

Screams from the monster ripped through the air, exploding into the silence. Announcing to every other demon that we were here.

So maybe whatever the snakes were in the pit, were harmful to demons?

Demons are the only thing that can kill another of their kind, Lilith said.

I wanted to run. But one wrong step and I had no doubt we'd be in another pit. "Into the house, here." I breathed the words and we hurried into the house closest to us, leaping through an open window, avoiding the sharp edges of glass left behind.

I wasn't sure that the house would be any better. But it would give us a moment of respite while we figured out where to go next. We scurried through the empty main floor, to a set of stairs and were up them in a flash to the higher level. I pressed myself against a far wall and let myself breathe.

"If there are traps like that everywhere," Maks said

softly, "there is no way to go faster. With one exception."

He looked pointedly at Lila.

She frowned. "I can't do this alone. And Asag would just have three of us then."

He nodded. "I know. He's given us a time limit that is impossible to meet by foot. I also know that you can carry Zam. The two of you can get to Asag."

I was shaking my head even as he nodded. "I said I wasn't leaving you behind again."

"You aren't. I'm telling you to go," he said, his blue eyes serious. "I'll do my best to follow as fast as I can. But splitting up means that the numbers of those after us have to split up too. They expect us to stay together, right?"

My guts twisted at the thought of Maks on his own. Not that he wasn't strong, not that he wasn't smart, but these were demons in a demon city and they were hunting us down. Or at least most of them were. "What about your guide? The demon hunter?"

Maks looked over his shoulder and gave a quick nod. "He's here. He'll help me." He closed his eyes and then nodded. "Lila, what if I freed the younglings? Would they help us fight?"

Lila grimaced. "I don't know. If you decide to let them loose, they'll be hungry, and you'd make a tasty meal. You'd be better off to find a way to open all the cages at once."

Maks grunted. "Then that's what we'll do. We'll

focus on the dragons as we make our way to the castle. You focus on Asag. I'll meet you there."

I wanted to shift back to two legs and hold Maks tight. I settled for another head butt and licking his cheek. He wrapped a front paw around me and tugged me tight to his chest. "It will be okay, Zam. We take the challenges, we face them, we'll come out on top."

Cat love, it's weird but it works.

"Don't do anything stupid," I said. "And promise me we will finally do something that Indiana Jones never would have. Something quiet. Like . . . going on vacation." I didn't even fully know what a vacation was —I'd certainly never had one. But the idea was nice. Drinks. Lazing about with the ones you loved and that was about it, right?

He tugged both me and Lila in tight with his longer front legs, holding us for the space of a heartbeat. "Go, fly out the window. Stay high, I'll do the same as best I can to stay off the ground. Use the houses and avoid the traps."

Lila gave a soft cry. "Toad, you better not end up in the pot."

He chirped, a very distinct caracal sound, and I realized it could pass for a rabisu if you didn't know better. "They're going to have to catch me first, Lila."

Maks didn't wait for us to leave him—maybe so I wouldn't have to break my word. He bounded down the length of the room and leapt out the far window, to the rooftop, the tip of his tail disappearing in a flash.

The silence was deafening. "We should go," Lila said. "Time is ticking."

"Yeah." I bobbed my head, ignoring the hurt wrapping around me. I knew Maks was strong and fast and smart. We'd both survived so much, so many close calls and yet I knew that our luck wouldn't last forever. And that was what scared me. We'd used up a lot of luck, just getting this far. We'd had help from so many, and now we were on our own.

I hurried over to the window ledge. Lila wrapped her claws around my upper body and swooped out the window, coasting for a moment before she had to start pumping her wings. Even like this, the time frame would be tight. And that was assuming we wouldn't run into anything else that would slow us down.

"Stay within the fog," I said. "Then he can't see us."

"Then we can't see either," she pointed out, but she did fly into the fog.

"You can sense Fen? Just fly for him," I said.

Lila flew for hours through the cold, damp fog, before she began to falter. My fur was soaked, and droplets fell from us both. I fed her my strength through our bond but even that was not going to be enough to get us all the way to the castle.

She kept on, her wings slowing and we began to droop in the sky, lower and lower until we were breaking through the fog.

"We need to rest," I whispered and gave her

another shot of energy. My eyes drooped but she was able to get us back into the fog.

For just that moment though, I'd thought I'd seen movement below us. The demons still? Most likely, though I had no idea how they'd tracked us.

"We can't stop," Lila said, powering us through the thick fog, veering around another rooftop. "They need us. I'll go till I drop. That's all there is to it."

Once more we slid below the fog cover. Below us I watched as shadows slid and slithered between the houses, down alleys, and always toward us.

"I've got nothing left to give, Lila." Even though I was not doing the work, all that energy I'd given her had drained me.

"Then we fly lower is all," Lila whispered.

Out of the fog we fell. I don't think it was any better. Now we passed cages of dragons, heard their whimpering and moans of pain. Those moments I felt Lila truly falter—and not out of exhaustion. We would both push till we dropped for them alone. For Reyhan and Fen.

But that would do our friends no good.

"They don't need us unable to save them because we're knackered." I flicked my tail toward a tall tower that was to our right, fog curling up it like a ribbon. There didn't seem to be any doorways near the bottom and there was a series of windows way up high.

So maybe nothing was in there?

One could hope. "There. We rest for a bit. Have something from the saddlebags."

Lila tipped her wings and took us toward the tower. She let me go on the ledge first and I scrambled into the circular room. She followed a moment later, but I was already sniffing the air, trying to make sure we had the all-clear.

There was nothing. No scent of another animal, human, or monster. No smell of food, fire . . . just emptiness. Good, right? Yeah, my thoughts too.

"Is this safe?" Lila whispered. "Forget it, I don't care. I just want to close my eyes for a few minutes."

From below the tower came a series of chirps.

We both pulled ourselves up over the lip of the window to look down. The demons posing as rabisu had followed us far more closely than I realized. The shadows further out slowly turned into more rabisu right in front of me. More and more.

And they were climbing up the freaking tower, digging their claws into the stone.

Lila shook her head. "Deep, hollow, treacherous and full of guile. They just do not give up."

I didn't look away from the rabisu. "*Richard III*."

"Damn it."

I smiled but the smile faltered quickly. We could not keep going like this. Not on foot, and not in the air. And how were they finding us this far up, away from them? It was if they were hunting by scent.

"Lilith, is that possible?" I asked.

What?

I knew she'd been there, in my thoughts, I'd felt her touch inside my mind. "That they are hunting by scent."

No. You have something they can sense, you fool, it is making it easy to track you. Your mate will not have near as much trouble as you.

"We have a few minutes before we have to fly," I said, not yet ready to tell Lila what Lilith was saying. "Let's think about this while you have a chance to rest." As I spoke I let some more of my energy trickle into her, sneaky like. Because I knew she would protest. But at that moment, she was doing the lion's share of the work. We'd flown for hours. And we weren't even a quarter of the way to the castle.

"What is there to think about? We have to go anyway, it's not like there's a better way to get to his damn castle," she grumbled. I sat on the window ledge so I could keep an eye on the rabisu, but also so I could look toward the castle. Also, so I could discuss this with Lilith.

"What thing?" I muttered.

Me. Her laughter was sharp. *They sense me. And you aren't going to let me go, are you? I thought not. So as long as you carry little old me, you're royally screwed.*

I held my breath, feeling her words sink further into me. For all that she was a demon and a liar, her words felt true. They fit with what was happening.

How in the seven hells were we supposed to get to

Asag without flying straight across? We needed the speed of Balder, but there was no way he could miss every snake pit, every rabisu. Every other danger that Asag had put in place to protect his sorry ass.

The main road that ran straight from the outskirts of Trevalon, through the main gates and to the castle, was perfect for an army. But it was blocked completely from the front. And there was no way to get Balder to it any other way.

I spoke my thoughts out loud, "Do you think that the rabisu demons would actually kill us, Lila? He wants me, we know that. What if we bargained with them?"

"What are you asking me? I'm tired, my brain doesn't want to believe you are saying what I think you might be saying. Because that would be stupid," she snapped. "You are not going to *let* them take you."

She was right, it was stupid to think of putting myself into their hands deliberately. I sighed and looked down at the climbing rabisu demons. They were chirping away, but there was no mind fuck like the last time. I wasn't seeing them as Maks coming to claim me. Because they weren't actually rabisu.

Just demons.

Ha! Yeah, just demons.

"We only have a couple minutes," I said. "And I can only think of one other person to ask."

"You mean, the demon strapped to your back?" Lila asked. "You think that's a good idea?"

"If she wants to kill her brother, she needs me to get to him," I pointed out. "If she wants even a chance, she needs to help me get to him." I threw the words out like the challenge they were meant to be.

Nothing.

The damn demon was silent now. Of course she was. I looked at Lila and shook my head.

And the best way to talk to Lilith, if she wasn't feeling in the mood, was to hold the handle of the sword. Which meant I would have to shift again . . . I forced myself to walk back through the doorway in my mind. At the edge of the physical change, it felt like I was pushing through mud, fighting to get back to my human shape. With a cry, I stumbled back to two legs, then went to my knees, breathing hard.

My muscles seized and danced and I struggled to get past the reaction. There was no time to coddle myself, though.

I reached back and took hold of the sword handle. "Lilith."

What? she grumbled through me. *You've proven you can beat me, now you want my help?*

I gritted my teeth and forced myself to pull the sword free. The first rabisu demon stuck its head up over the lip of the window. Two steps and I swung, cutting its head off.

Lilith moaned. *Do it again. Tasting the blood of another demon is so very lovely.*

"Lilith, we need a way to get to Asag with speed, or

you will never get your chance to kill him," I said. She had said that one demon could kill another.

Her sigh rippled into my hand and up my arm. *You're playing his game. You are on his chess board. You have to change the rules now if you want a chance to beat him.*

I frowned; another rabisu demon stuck its head up and I removed it from its neck and shoulders with a swift slice. "What do you mean I have to change the rules? That's not how this works!"

Her laughter filled the room and Lila hissed.

You are in his final challenge, yes? The last thing you must face before you get to him. He gave you a time limit to save your friends. That's what's driving you. Do you have nothing that he wants?

I repeated her words to Lila. "What does he want that we have? Me?"

Lila's eyes went wide. "You think he'd want his sister back?"

It was Lilith's turn to hiss. *Do not offer me to him!*

Yeah. That answer was a little too quick. Which meant that was exactly what *she* wanted me to do. I rolled the sword in my hand and winked at Lila, hoping she understood that I knew what I was doing. "What if we offered Lilith to him? You think he'd take her? I mean, she's destined to kill him, so if she was in his hands, maybe he'd think he was safe?"

Lilith began screeching, the sound filling the room. But under it, I could just feel the edge of her glee.

She thought she'd fooled me. Again.

Lila tipped her head at me. "I'd be glad to get rid of the screeching harpy."

I smiled and gave her a quick nod. "I think I'm going to make him a deal. One that he can't refuse."

Of course, making a deal with a demon was no better than making a deal with the devil.

But here I went, gambling once more.

EIGHT

He ran west through the demon city, sticking close to the building edges where there was less likely to be a sand snake pit for him. Roshawn jogged in his spectral form close to him.

"I don't believe this was how the prophecies went," he muttered. "Where is the black hornless unicorn? Where is the little dragon? Where is Vahab? None of this is making sense to me."

Maks wanted to laugh at Roshawn. Not because it was truly funny . . . "Zam has a way of doing things," he said softly. "She will get the job done, and then you will ask how and she will shrug and say she just did what she had to do. I don't think . . ." He dodged a clawed hand reaching for him that shot out of a doorway. "I don't think that she will follow the rules. And I think that Asag is going to regret ever crossing her."

Even as he said that he felt in his belly that it was true. He let out a chirp, and a few of the faceless strange monsters came from his left. He skirted further to the right. Up a sidewall and onto a rooftop. His chirps seemed to confuse them.

The houses were all abandoned as far as he could see. "What is this place? Trevalon is empty, deserted. But here, there are homes everywhere."

Roshawn sighed. "It was once the home of the Jinn. Our seat of power before . . . before Asag came. Before he began his rise to power. Once we were all wiped out, or pushed out, he turned it over to the demons that he brought with him, and it became one of his safeguards."

A shudder slid down Maks's back as he looked at the buildings. He found himself searching for a speck in the darkened sky ahead of him. But there was no sign of Lila or Zam. By the number of hours that had passed, it should be mid-day, the brightest amount of sun shining down on them. The fog still lay in heavy patches to the east, and the sky was as dark as any cloud-filled night.

"It is too far to make it in twenty-four hours," Roshawn said softly. "That bastard knew it would separate you, and force you to run harder than you should through this maze of monsters and demons." He swept his hand outward. Not far from Maks stood one of the dragon cages. He'd passed by several, but their occupants had been quiet. Lifeless except for the occasional rattling breath.

Not that he didn't want to let them out, but Lila's words had stuck with him. They would see him as food, not as a friend.

"They are on their last bits of energy, these ones." Roshawn waved his hand toward the dragons. "Another one or two power pulls and they will shrivel up into nothing."

Nothing. Dead and gone.

Maks found himself sliding down the rooftop to the cage that held a medium-sized dragon. He dropped onto the top of it, the cage swinging under his weight. "Friend. I'm going to free you." This was as good an opportunity as any. It might give Asag something to think about if Maks started freeing all the dragons he could. And it would cut the demon's power.

"That's a good idea," Roshawn said. "Pissing Asag off and stealing his energy source might draw him out of his castle. But try not to get eaten."

He shifted back to two legs, lay flat on his belly and took a moment. His ability to shift back and forth was strong, but he was exhausted, and already he was feeling the ache in his bones. Drawing a deep, slow breath, he peered over the edge of the cage to the dragon inside. Hues of blue scales, dirty from its own filth, a thick ridge of spinal scales and a pair of iridescent pearly-colored wings were all he could see. He watched for a moment to make sure that the dragon was indeed alive.

Finally, the belly lifted in breath, sliding out of the dragon in a shudder. "You're just a kid, Asag did this to you," Maks said softly. "I'd like to let you out."

A long low hiss rumbled out of the dragon. "I'll kill him myself."

Feminine, low, and very, *very* pissed off.

"Happy to help you with that." Maks found the latch of the cage. The lock was solid. Using the tip of one of his knives, he worked the lock over and had it free and open in a matter of seconds. "But I think that it's best that you fly west. Go to the Dragon's Ground. Your family waits for you there."

Jewel-toned blue eyes lifted to his. "I have no family."

"You were stolen as an egg," Maks said. "And we are here to set you free."

Those eyes slid over him. "You."

"Me."

"And what army?"

He grinned. "Well, if I could find a way to make the path clear, I could bring through an army of shifters and unicorns that are quite looking forward to killing Asag and his golems and send the demons back to their realm. Perhaps you could convince and free a few of the other dragons here? We could work together."

The dragon pulled herself out of the cage and up on top of it, next to him. She was about six feet long, and slender, not unlike Fen. But he could see that was not her natural state. Ribs and edges of her bones peeked out all over. Her skin clung to her body, showing every breath she took.

She was starving. "Let's get off this cage," he said, turned and leapt to the roof closest. He wasn't as agile on two legs, but it would do.

She followed. "Do you have a name?"

"Maks."

"Seven, that's mine," she said softly. "Short for seven, seven, seven. They give us numbers when they stick us in the cages."

His stomach rolled. She had a number, not a name. He didn't have much food on him, but the bits of jerky he had he offered to her. She took the pieces carefully, her eyes closing as she chewed it down. "If we free more of the other dragons, that would—"

"More than that, I know a dragon who could make it so your army could come through . . . I think," she said around her jerky. "He can control the ground. He could rumble it so that you could see all the traps, right? He might even be able to flatten the buildings, knock the main walls down. Open the gates."

Flatten the buildings. Then they'd have a clear path to Asag. Perfect for Bryce and the unicorns to come through. He knew that Zam didn't want her brother involved, but Maks would do anything to keep his mate safe. She was his priority.

"How far is he? Which cage is he in?"

She shook her head. "I don't know. But he's our best bet. We were hatched together. So I'd recognize his smell."

Maks nodded, his decision made in that moment. Lila and Zam could keep heading toward the keep, toward Fen and Reyhan. He would work with Seven and find this ground-shaking dragon. One of their paths had to work.

They had to or not only were Reyhan and Fen lost, but all of them.

"I'm going to start opening more cages, those closest around here," he said. "You rest—"

"No, I'm feeling better already." She wobbled as she stood, using her wings to help steady herself. "No point in opening the cages of those who can't help. It'll just slow us down."

She wasn't wrong, and yet Maks could feel the pull to just open as many cages as he could.

"Okay, we find this ground-shaker first, then we open as many cages as we can." He paused. "How long between the blue lightning that he used on you?"

"That's how he takes our energy," she said. "He pulls on us once or twice a day. It depends on his mood. Never more than that."

Never more than that. "So maybe twelve hours?"

She bobbed her head. "Maybe."

Maks turned his back on the young dragon and slipped out the window. "Then we have time to find this ground shaker." He wasn't sure they had time at all. Not at all.

But that didn't mean he wasn't going to use the time given to them. He shifted back to four legs, wobbling, groaning as his body shuddered. Seven bunted his side with her nose. "I thought I'd lost my mind, watching a cat jump onto my cage and then for that cat to become a man. Is this . . . are you a demon?" She reeled, scuttling back from him, then sniffed the air. "You don't smell like a demon.

Maks shook his head. "No, I'm half Jinn, half shifter."

She sucked in a breath. "Half Jinn? What is that?"

"Doesn't matter," he said. "Come on, if you're ready, let's go."

She tucked in close to him, and the two of them used the rooftops to traverse their way to the next closest cage. Before he could even see the inhabitant of it, Seven was shaking her head. "No, that's not him."

They were on the third cage when the sound of footsteps tugged at his ears. He looked back to see not golems as he'd thought, or even the strange chirping creatures. The mindless monsters of Asag were bad. But this? This new threat was far, far worse. Even if it was, in fact, not new at all.

"What are those?" Seven curled closer to him, showing her age. Despite her size, she was just a kid.

The men—and Maks used that term loosely—were dressed in armor, their leather skin peeking out here and there, their lizard fazes looking about, tongues flicking in and out as they tasted the air. Hunting.

Hunting for them?

Asag was pulling out all the stops. Next would be the undead of the Jinn and they'd be rounding out all that he, Zam and Lila had faced so far. These demons were dicks.

Even as he thought it, the sound of wings came from the distance.

"Fuck," he muttered under his breath. He did not want to be right about this.

"What do we do?" Seven whispered.

"We keep looking for your friend. As fast as we can." He bunted her with his head, gently, to get her moving. They scuttled across the tops of the buildings, but the sound of her claws was just enough to draw the attention of those they didn't want.

A guttural scream went up through the air and Maks took off, full speed, fully expecting Seven to stick with him. The way Lila would have.

Only a few bounds into his flight, and he realized he'd left her behind. He circled back as an arrow shot past his side, skimming his fur as he leapt between buildings.

"Seven!"

He scanned the rooftop, seeing her curled tight to a chimney that was crumbling. "I can't," she whispered. "I'm afraid."

He rushed to her side. "What does your friend look like? I'll find him."

She cringed at the sound of banging and crashing in the home below them. "They're coming."

"Tell me what he looks like," Maks urged her. "Then I will lead them all away from you, okay?"

Her eyes were wide, her lips trembling around her rows of teeth that could gut one of those leathered-up lizard men in a flash. But she couldn't with all that fear riding her.

"He's a deep brown, with green spots all over him. Tiny wings and amber eyes," she whispered. "His name is Two."

"Two. Got it. Stay hidden, find food if you can and slowly make your way out when you have enough strength. Release other dragons if you can do it and they are strong enough to fight." He butted his head against hers and took off again. Not across the rooftops. But down and into the house.

Roshawn jogged beside him, flickering in and out of view. "You are throwing yourself into danger for a dragon you don't even know."

"She's a child, and she and the others will die if we don't do something," Maks snarled as he encountered the first lizard man. The spear the man held was tipped with a wicked blade, curved on four edges.

The spear was thrown hard, but not accurate, and Maks leapt over it, down and between the lizard man's legs. The stairs were littered with more of the same creatures. The same as they'd faced months ago.

Maks snarled and turned, running for the far end of the upper hall, straight toward the broken-out window.

Leap and the net will appear, that was his only thought as he dove out the window, stretching with his front paws so he missed all the broken glass. He looked down as he jumped. He would reach the far side of the street at least.

Hopefully there was no sand snake pit waiting for him.

To make sure he had the lizard men's attention, he landed at the edge of a pit, spun and yowled up at them, hissing and spitting. And then he waited as they thundered back down the stairs. A quick glance up at the roof showed him a pair of jeweled eyes looking back at him.

They'd not seen Seven.

He bobbed his head in her direction, flicking his ears and then he was off, running down the street, lizard men behind him. Chirps coming in from ahead of him. Snake pits everywhere.

And a dragon named Two to find.

NINE

ZAM

L ilith was trying very hard to contain her glee that I'd fallen for her trap—that I'd *believed* that she didn't want to be taken by her brother. Of course she wanted me to trade her to her brother, Asag. That would allow her to take him over—assuming she was strong enough. I wasn't about to let that happen. But if she thought he'd take the deal, it was worth a try. Maybe to buy us more time.

"Asag," I shouted his name, "I have a new deal for you. What would you give to have Lilith back in your hands?"

Lila crept up my leg, over my torso and wrapped herself around my neck. "Terrible damn idea, Zam."

She could very well be right. But I had to try something. I had to try and get us close to the palace. I had to make sure that Reyhan and Fen didn't get killed.

It didn't take long for his booming voice to answer. "What deal are you thinking, Zamira of the desert?"

"I'll bring Lilith to you," I said. "And I'll give her to you freely . . . if you take the twenty-four-hour time limit off and remove your demons from chasing us. Keep our friends alive, and I'll gladly hand over the blade that holds your sister's soul when I meet you face to face." I mean, assuming that she had a soul. Maybe essence was a better word. Whatever the case, I would hand the shithead over.

There was a heavy pause in the air, the sound of the rabisu demons halted and I knew that they were waiting on his command.

"Why would I do that when I can just take the blade from you when I choose to?"

"He makes a point," Lila said softly. "Even if he is a jackass."

My jaw ticked. I thought about what Pazuzu had said before we'd left, about what Mamitu had said about Asag's weakness. And suddenly together the two made sense. Asag loved to be entertained. That a part of this challenge was because he was bored out of his mind. Okay, maybe he hadn't said it quite like that. I took a breath.

"Because I will entertain you like no other trying to get to my friends. If they are dead, there is no reason for me to keep fighting. I'll just turn around and escape the way I slipped in. Right where Nico and Soleil showed me."

Another heavy pause; this one lasted far longer. Yup, I'd just thrown Nico and Soleil under the rolling rock headed our way.

I could almost feel him thinking, weighing his options. "Three days. You have three days to reach me. But I will not call off my friends." His laughter was smooth, as if he couldn't believe I'd have ever asked for that in the first place. But I'd had to try.

I breathed out a quiet sigh of relief. "Three days, and I will deliver you with Lilith."

Yup, I know that it sounded weird. But words were power, and I would not be one to be caught in a promise broken. Lila shot me a look and her eyes widened. She understood what I meant at least.

"You will entertain me, shifter, desert born, Zamira . . . you and your family will entertain me. And then you will belong to me until I see fit to kill you, fuck you, and eat your souls."

My blood chilled. Did he know that Bryce, Kiara and the others were waiting? Goddess damn Pazuzu to the end of the world. I'd not wanted my brother involved for this very reason.

"We three will entertain you. You can see us at all times from where you are if you remove the fog, so that should be easy." This was a guess, dependent on the fact that we hadn't been able to truly get ahead of anything.

Even as I spoke, the fog blew away, though the sky was still dark.

"Yes, all of you I can see." He laughed and the sound faded, as if he knew I would question what he meant. Fucker.

There was a beat of silence before my friend spoke up.

"I hate to say this, but I wish that Jasten and his two tag-alongs had stuck with us," Lila said, mumbling from inside my hood, her jaw cracking with a yawn. It was a wonder to me that she could tumble asleep when we were in the middle of all this. Then again . . . perhaps that was the trust between us.

I would protect her, no matter what, and would wake her only if I needed to.

Below us, the rabisu demons started up their chirping again. Sliding up the wall.

"You rest, Lila," I said, "and I'll do the heavy lifting. We'll take turns. I'll tackle the day; you take the night shift. We'll make it there in three days." We had to, there was no other option.

Thirty miles a day on foot was not impossible. It would be tough, but not impossible.

I swung out of the window and let myself drop straight down. My feet slammed into the first rabisu demon's head, peeling it off the wall, even as it slowed my fall. It hit the ground first and I landed next to it in a crouch, pulled Lilith from my back and sliced off the rabisu demon's head.

A blast of heat rolled up and around us from the body. That was different. "Lilith, what is that about?"

None of your business.

Fine. It didn't really matter to me as long as I could cut their heads off.

I grunted and turned down the street in front of me, staying close to the building edges. Away from the center where there were more likely to be traps set up. I gripped the sword handle lightly. Whatever power was inside of Lilith, it did far more damage to the demons than anyone really had thought possible. Something that I think Lilith knew, but didn't want to tell me.

You still hold me, Lilith said. *You think yourself stronger than me now?*

"No." I breathed out the word as a rabisu demon launched itself at me from behind a building. The only warning I had was the scuttle of sand under its feet.

Then why do you hold me still?

"Can you not see?" I snapped as I rammed the blade into another rabisu.

Actually no, I cannot. I am after all trapped in a sword, you idiot.

I turned and jumped through a broken window, into the lower levels of one of the homes. I had an idea, one that would save me from another near miss with a pit of sand snakes or whatever else the asshat Asag had up his sleeve. I searched the room, quickly finding the hardened leftovers, the same as the other house. Opening my hip satchel, I grabbed the mummified fruit and dumped them into my bag.

"You said it yourself. Demons are the only ones

who can kill demons. It's why your brother wants you back. So you don't get used against him. But while you are with me," I paused, sensing something at my back. I spun, swinging the sword out, cutting the dark shadow completely in half. The shadowy demon writhed and split apart, its essence dissipating. "We are going to kill every demon we can."

She had no answer to that.

I flexed my hand around Lilith's handle. I knew that she was just waiting for me to let my guard down. Fucker. The whole lot of demons were fuckers.

Back out into the street, I pulled what was likely a pomegranate at some point, and bowled it down the street. It rolled along well, relatively straight, and then the sand fell away from it and there came a bellow of . . . something big.

My heart clenched. "Giants." There was only one sound that reverberated through your bones at that decibel. "Demons that shifted into giants. What the actual fuck?"

Lila mumbled something that I didn't quite hear. I jogged toward the pit opening, skimming it along the side, but I couldn't resist taking a quick look.

Yup, a giant all right. And a whoppsy big one. The giant stared back at me, gnashing her teeth. She could have been the doppelganger of the queen I'd dealt with what seemed like a thousand years before. Okay, more like a hundred, but so long it seemed that I could scarcely remember the person I'd been then.

"They trap you?" I asked on the off chance it was an actual giant, and not a demon impersonating one.

"Imma wanna eat eat you!" the beefy bitch bellowed. The smell off her mouth was rotten, as foul as the green on her teeth. But the glint of her eyes screamed demon. So not another real giant, at least.

She leapt up and her finger skimmed just below the surface of the pit. I hurried along until I came to a new street. I rolled an apple this time. Nothing. I jogged down the path that the fruit had left in the sand. Just in case.

It took about fifteen minutes for me to clue in that there was no more chirping.

No more rabisu demons?

Of course, they might have discussed the fact that I was using Lilith on their friends, and actually demolishing them.

I wasn't worried that I'd be left alone. Nope, not for a second. Not if Asag wanted his entertainment. "He thinks I won't be able to banish him," I breathed, thinking out loud. "Did he let me get this far for the sake of . . . boredom?"

I kept on using the trick with the fruit. I dodged two more giants and another sand snake pit. Go me. I paused at the next intersection. The obvious choice would be to keep going north. I went west.

A gong sounded as I stepped onto the western road. "Lila, hang on," I said softly.

She mumbled something from under my hood and

tightened herself around my neck. I tossed an apple down the street—no sand traps.

I jogged forward, confident that I was good. A bellow rolled out from my left and I twisted, turning as flash of white fur caught at my eyes.

"Impossible." I breathed the word as I went to my knees and the massive white bear went over my head. Impossible because the white bear belonging to the witch of the north was dead. Even knowing that it was a demon impersonating the white bear, it didn't matter. The fear struck true, right through my heart.

The big asshole scrabbled on the far side of the dirt road, and I had nowhere to go but run. Run and hope that the thundering feet of the bear behind me shook the sand traps loose as we got close to them.

I took off, arms and legs pumping hard. Thinking about . . . "Lila, I'm going to shift!"

It was a terrible idea; I had no energy left. But I couldn't outrun the bear on two legs. I could on four. Okay, I hoped I could outrun it on four.

Between one stride and the next I let my body slide between that doorway in my mind. I didn't turn into a house cat, though; I took my jungle cat form. My vision fluttered and my heart seemed to beat off rhythm. Gulping a breath and steadying myself as best I could, I leaned into my running. With a powerful surge I leapt ahead of the bellowing, swatting bear.

"It's like every damn nightmare we've ever fought!"

I yelped out as I skidded around a corner and bounced off the edge of a brick house. I felt claws pass by my long tail and that gave me another boost of speed. When the adrenaline wore off, I was going to be in trouble.

I needed help.

I hoped that Maks was doing better than we were, out there in the demon city. Freeing dragons.

In and out of buildings we blasted, down long strips of quiet roads. Quiet except for the bellowing bear at my back.

I needed to find a place to hide, or get away from the bear. Sure, Lilith could have killed him, but the bear's reach was far longer than mine. I couldn't risk the fight, not if I didn't have to.

Where though? The rooftops again?

My eyes caught the glimmer of a crescent moon etched into the door to my right.

The same crescent moon that Soleil had mentioned.

I didn't even think about it, I just dove through the door. I kicked the door shut behind me with a back foot, not that I thought it would actually help me. The white bear was no joke. I'd nearly died fighting him the first time.

And it had been the flail more than me that had finished the beast off.

To think that a wave of nostalgia flowed over me at the thought of the murderous, but relatively simple weapon would have made me laugh if I hadn't been fighting for every breath.

I swept the room, looking for another clue.

There it was, another crescent moon was etched into the frame of the door that led to the back. I ran for it, and it took me into the busted-up kitchen. Herbs still hung from the rafters, scenting the air with their musty perfume.

Crescent moon, where was it? There had to be another one to lead me along.

"Lila, help me find a crescent moon!"

She clung to my back and pointed to my left. "There! In the brick!"

The fireplace had a small moon drawn into the ash. Good enough. I leapt into the dead fireplace as the bear burst through the window behind us. I spun and stared at him: slathering mouth, dead eyes, white fur flying as he locked on us.

Demon eyes. Calculating and more deadly than the white bear had ever been.

And then the space below me opened and we fell through.

I bit back the snarl that surged to the front of my mouth. Because I didn't fall far, only a few feet. The space above me disappeared as the trapdoor slammed shut. I took a breath, then sneezed.

A voice I did not know whispered, "Bless you."

I froze. "Who the fuck is in here?"

"Not an enemy." A light bloomed and I spun on my

ass to find myself looking into the face of a tiny pixy. A fairy.

"Who are you?"

She shook her head, autumn colors flickering even in the light of her small lantern. "Doesn't really matter. I'm not here to cause you harm, just trying to find an ingredient for a spell." She sighed. "It wasn't here, in case you were wondering."

"I wasn't."

"Oh well, if you go back that way, you'll miss the trolls, and the gargoyles. But you'll still have to deal with the loose dragons." She fluttered around my head for a moment. "Assuming that you are going toward the palace? He has a lot of dragons there. And more demons, of course."

Lila had slipped off my back now and I pulled her close to me. I wasn't sure about this pixy; they could be trouble. "Yes, the palace is our goal. You . . . you've been there?"

Above us the bear scrabbled and clawed at the floorboards. We both looked up. She flipped the bear off. Even though we couldn't see him, I liked her better for it.

"Shitty place that. It's almost as bad as out here." She shrugged again and dipped sideways, her wings fluttering lightly. "But that's the way to the palace if you really want to go, the path is straight from here on out."

"That's handy," Lila said softly. "If you run the whole way, Zam . . ."

If I ran the whole way, we'd make it well within the deadline Asag had given us. I didn't trust him not to hurt Reyhan and Fen, even if I *did* make it within the timeline. But that didn't mean I wanted to give him more time with them than I had to.

The pixy narrowed her eyes. "You need a light? I'm leaving. This place is a serious shithole." She thrust the super tiny lantern toward me. There was no way I could take it with my jungle cat mitts. Lila scooped it from her, hanging it from the tip of her tail.

"Thanks. There's a bear out there," I said. "In case you were wondering what the clawing was all about." Even as I spoke, it went quiet above.

"No problem. I should be good to fly high now, it won't catch me," the pixy said. "If you don't mind lifting that false floor." She pointed at the spot I'd fallen through.

"Maybe we should wait a minute?" I said. "You know. Bear and all."

The pixy shook her head. "The demons give up quick. So, it'll be gone now. Trust me."

I didn't. But it was her life on the line, not mine.

Without another word I put my shoulders to it and pushed off with my back feet just enough that she could slip out. There was no sound of a bear, no smell of one either.

Had I lost my mind?

"How did you find this place?" Lila asked.

"The crescent moon was marked on the house." I padded forward, my eyes making out the way easily even with the small amount of light. "Lila, the demons are bringing up everything we've faced since our first journey together to the Witch's Reign." I shuddered thinking about everything we'd dealt with. The monsters. The heartbreak.

She paused and held up the lantern. "Then we know we can face it all and win. Right? We did it once, we do it again."

Only I wasn't so sure it would be that easy. I could feel the fear clawing at me, just the same as the fear of facing the white bear the first time. It was as if there was some connection to how the rabisu could make you see your loved ones, to let them close. A type of magic that made you feel that fear even knowing that it wasn't really the same monsters.

Then again, they'd still kill us straight up. Or would they? Asag wanted entertainment; he couldn't have that if we were dead.

More than that, he wanted me for other things. I shuddered.

I closed my eyes a moment and thought about the last few minutes. Bear. Giants. Rabisu. "It's not all in my mind though, you saw them too?"

Lila curled the tip of her tail through the lantern handle and held it just over her back. "I'm not saying you didn't see it. My eyes were closed. Maybe whatever spell it is affects only your visual memories?"

Surprisingly, Lilith was the one who gave me the answer. Her words rattled me in a way I didn't think was possible. Because . . . it meant we were in for the worst ride of our lives.

I told you, you fool! They grab your worst memories and use them to drive you mad. That is what instabilismori demons do. Did you not hear me the first time?

"Lila, the dangers are real, but . . . he pulls them from your memories, and from mine. From our darkest moments. He is going to make us face our deepest fears again and again."

Lila let out a soft groan. "Please tell me you're joking."

I hurried up my steps. "I don't think demons joke, and honestly, even if Lilith is lying—which she could be. Does it matter? We will face what we face. And that is it. If the monsters and challenges ahead of us are the worst that we've already seen, then we can do it again. If we've done it once, we can do it again. Just like you said."

Yeah, that's what I said out loud, but in my heart of hearts, I knew we were in trouble. Because if every challenge we'd faced up to this point was coming back to haunt us, all at the same time, we were about to be in a world of hurt like never before.

TEN

MAKS

He bolted through the streets, bouncing off the walls as the lizard men of the desert followed him, throwing spears and arrows, popping out of buildings, and reaching for him with a speed that he *almost* couldn't avoid.

"This is fucking bullshit," he snarled as he used a window ledge, bouncing off it in order to dodge a lance that swung toward his head. He could have stopped to fight, but that would not help him find the dragon that might be able to *actually* help the bullshit situation he was in. Bullshit. Complete and utter bullshit. It was the only word he had for all this.

Maks scrambled up a brick wall beside a house and hopped over it into what had once been a garden if the overgrown brush and weeds was any indication.

Across from him was another dragon's cage, hanging off the edge of the house, dragon slumped with a leg dangling out the side. Deep red scales on the leg.

Would that make for some fiery dragon to help him out? An eye rolled his way and the scaled claw swatted at him as he drew close, a whine deep in its throat. A plume of fire followed and Maks dropped to his belly as he scooted into the house, through the rooms and away from the now bellowing dragon. His luck had been with him when he'd freed the little blue dragon.

The others he'd seen had either been close to death or looked at him like he would make a great appetizer.

At least Seven hadn't tried to eat him. Considering the dragons were all emaciated, it wasn't an unreasonable reaction to seeing food run by.

He slid into a small room on the bottom floor of the house and pinned himself up against a wall. There were no sounds of pursuit, and he took a moment to catch his breath. To think about just how he was going to find this earth-shaking dragon.

He needed a bird's-eye view of the city. A map. Something.

"I need Lila's help," he whispered to himself. Of course she was with Zam, but that didn't mean he couldn't wish for her.

Roshawn materialized next to him, crouched down and tapped a hand on the floor. "You have my help. What do you need?"

Maks glared at him. "Yeah? Go find the dragon I

need then. Seeing as you can walk about without anyone but me seeing you."

Roshawn laughed at him. "I am attached to you, fool. I can't walk about freely. But I can answer questions."

Of course he couldn't help. Maks sighed and laid his head on his paws. He needed to think this through. There had to be a way to find the dragon that could shake the earth. Two. He needed to find number two.

His head snapped up. They were numbered, all the dragons were numbered. So, could that mean that they were put in their cages in the same way?

He scrabbled around the room, looking for a piece of paper. On the shelf at the back were several old books. He grabbed at one well worn, larger book and clawed it onto the floor.

As much as he hated to do it, he needed hands and fingers for what he was thinking. He shifted back to two legs and stayed on his knees a moment, breathing hard. Back and forth too many times, he was going to wear himself out.

"You have thoughts in that head of yours?" Roshawn asked.

"Maybe you can help with this." Maks flipped the book open to the back and pulled a mostly blank page free. "I need something to write with, help me search the room."

Roshawn did as he asked, which was something. "You know, you could be asking me all sorts of important things. Like how to remove the demon, perhaps? This was my home, once, long ago. I can help with traversing the town."

"We have got to get to him first." Maks let his fingers travel over the same shelf where the book had rested. "Which at this rate is going to be . . ." No, he wouldn't say impossible. "Difficult."

"Well, if you do get to him, I'm not going to be able to give you the information then. So I'll just tell you now."

Maks saw the pencil just before his fingers brushed against it. Charcoal tipped, it would work well enough for what he planned.

"Tell me then, while I draw this out, and you can correct me if there are obvious mistakes," he said softly. He wasn't a wiz with maps, but he could do a basic layout. One that would help him navigate in the right direction at least if he could find a few landmarks to work from.

He sketched the walls, where they'd come in underneath, and then roughly where he'd found Seven more to the eastern side of the city. But had he crossed the main strip, the one that was wide and protected? No, no he hadn't. He drew that strip in too, grimacing. Because what if Two was on the *other* side of that main drag? Would he be able to get across it? How was it protected on this side of the demon city?

Questions for later.

Moving quietly, creeping through the house, he

made his way up to the second floor, then the third and out onto the roof. Sitting in the alcove of the window, he looked out over the city spread in front of him.

"I think you aren't really paying attention," Roshawn said from behind him.

Maks sketched quickly, keeping things simple. Marking the houses, streets and cages that he could see, trying to find solid landmarks. Like the massive gargoyle sitting on the peak of what looked like a place of worship. "I'm listening."

Roshawn huffed but then he began to speak. "Demons can't really be killed, young one. That is the main problem. They can be banished, they can be broken and chained. They can be stuffed into weapons like Lilith, but they cannot be killed. They are demons, they are not truly mortal. They exist because of the darkness in the world, and nothing else. As far as we know, the only thing that can truly kill a demon, is another demon. It's why they are so afraid of Asag. He could wipe them out if he chose."

Maks had to fight not to pause what he was doing. "So how do we deal with Asag? If we can't kill him, all we can do is banish him?"

Roshawn sighed and jumped up onto the roof with Maks. He spread his hands wide. "Do you think that he will go back to the demon realm when he's been living in this world? There is no way you or your woman are strong enough to send him back. Your best bet is to push him into an item. Contain him. Not unlike what was done to Lilith. That was a brilliant stroke of genius, if I may say so."

Maks did pause then. "But that means he is still here, and the possibility is that he could free himself. Just like Lilith found her way into Zam's hands, Asag could find his way into another's hands. Someone not good like Zam. Someone weak."

His almost mentor dipped his head. "I have put several demons into vessels, young one. That is what they considered killing when I was alive, and I let my people believe it so that they felt safer. But I believe that the demons know what I did now. And I believe that perhaps Asag is looking for ways to free some of those first demons. Demons that were incredibly fierce, and wild beyond even Asag's reckonings."

Maks found his body going very still as the thoughts tumbled through his head, fighting one another to come out of his mouth first. "I didn't walk across your grave, did I? You were waiting for me."

"Astute. I wondered if you'd realize that I need you to finish what was laid out before me." Roshawn turned to him. "Vahab and I were friends, and we worked together to bring Asag to his knees. He wasn't necessarily the most powerful demon, but he was the craftiest. We called him the Beast from the East, because he is like an animal. He is very good at surviving, at staying safe. He is taunting your woman because he is bored, but also because he does not believe she has any power to stop him." Roshawn paused. "We confined him to the castle. He cannot physically leave; it is why he sends out his golems and other demons to do his dirty work for him."

Maks looked out over the massive city. Miles and miles of it. The palace at the northern end was huge even at the distance that he was from it. Which meant up close and personal, it would be even bigger.

"So how do we stuff him into a vessel?" Maks asked. "We've been stripped of our magic."

Roshawn crouched beside him. "Correct. But I have not. My magic still resides in my essence."

That drew a frown on Maks's face. "What are you saying?"

"You shared a body before, with the Jinn masters. Would you be willing to do it again, if it meant stopping Asag?"

It was Maks's turn to huff. "How do you think that will help? When I shared my body before, I had magic of my own. So it wasn't like they brought magic to the table with them."

He went back to his map making. He'd drawn it all as small as he could so that he could expand the map further. If needed. Who the hell was he kidding? This was going to be like finding a camel whisker in the desert.

For a moment he closed his eyes and let himself feel the connection between himself and Zam. Why had he left her? And in such a hurry? Not that splitting up was a terrible idea, but they'd just finished saying that they would stick it out together. That nothing would part them this time. And then he'd felt this incredible urge to go. To run toward Asag on his own.

He turned and looked at Roshawn. "You old fucker, you are influencing me, aren't you?"

Roshawn shrugged and smiled. "Your mate has her path, and you have yours. You'll find each other on the other side. One way or another."

Maks let out a low growl. "The other side? You mean when we're dead?"

Again, he shrugged. "Most likely. You don't actually think that you'll survive all this? I appreciate the effort, I really do. You have the heart of a demon hunter, I can see it, as does your mate." Roshawn pointed at the castle. "But you aren't going to be able to stop the Beast from the East. Not the way you think. We trapped him all those years ago. Now we need to finish the job. I was killed in trapping him thus far."

"Even with Lilith?" Maks asked. He wasn't angry, not really. Just . . . tired and frustrated.

"Lilith will turn on your mate the second she has the chance," Roshawn said softly. "She is a demon too, and she has been trapped for a very long time. I believe she is playing possum, as the saying goes."

Maks took a look at his map, and then at the nearest cage. He couldn't let Roshawn's words stop him. "We need to move. We've been still too long."

Even as he spoke there was the soft sound of something moving up the stairs behind them. Maks tucked the map under his shirt, and moved down the roofline, leapt across to the building closest to him, and from there shimmied down a chain hanging from the roof. It rattled twice and he winced, feeling eyes swing his way from inside the buildings. He was not as quiet on two legs as four, but he was exhausted. He dropped to the ground in a crouch, then pinned himself against the wall.

With his back flat against the wall, he waited.

A snarl erupted from above him, the blow of a heavy breath of air, then the sound of leathery wings cut through the air.

"The dead Jinn." Maks mouthed the words, he didn't even truly say them out loud as he watched the twisted body of the Jinn that Marsum had retained control of, even after death. He didn't want to know how or why it was here.

If what Lilith had told Zam was correct, this was because he feared the dead Jinn almost more than anything else. In part because he'd believed for so long that would be his destiny. To be a monster controlled by Marsum once his use alive was done.

"He's using your fears against you," Roshawn said, confirming what Lilith had said. He of course didn't bother to lower his voice. "That's one of his gifts. To take the things you've faced, and turn them against you again. That's what these particular demons do."

What were Zam and Lila facing then? The Emperor? Giants? Dragons?

"You can still help them, your mate and your soul partner," Roshawn said. "You can. Let me help you help them."

There was a hypnotic quality to Roshawn's voice that Maks could feel digging under his skin. "Why are you trying to convince me so hard?"

Roshawn sighed and rubbed his hands over his face. "Because I was the one who should have stopped him all those years ago, and yet I didn't. I failed. I cannot rest until my quest is completed and I believe that you may be my last hope of doing so."

Again, pretty words, but Maks had been fooled before. "We do things my way. I'll think about what you're suggesting. But not until there is no other choice."

"Fair enough," Roshawn said. "So you want to find the dragon who shakes the earth? A dragon whose energy and magic have been drained from it every day? How exactly are you going to give it the energy to shake its tail, never mind an entire city?"

Maks was honest. "No fucking idea."

But he would figure it out. He had to.

ELEVEN

ZAM

The darkness of the tunnel was offset by the bobbing light that Lila clung to with the tip of her tail. Above my head, the ceiling just brushed the tip of my ears. Win number one for my jungle cat form.

I kept up a wicked pace, running flat out as Lila rode on my back, just at the base of my neck.

"You do not have a comfortable stride," she grumbled. "Not like Balder."

I didn't answer her. I was too focused on using every bit of energy I had to run as far and as fast as I could. I locked onto Reyhan's energy, feeling her grow a little closer with each leap I took.

Lila sighed. "I should be sleeping but it's impossible on your back. So. What, you egg?"

I smiled. *Macbeth*. Though I didn't say it out loud.

"Never mind, that's too easy. How about . . ." She paused for a moment. "How art thou out of breath when thou has breath to say to me that thou art out of breath? The excuse that thou dost make in this delay is longer than the tale thou dost excuse."

I huffed a single word. "Juliet."

"Damn it! And I thought you being out of breath, you'd maybe not get it. But suited to the moment, right?" Lila's pleasure with herself was obvious.

Another time I would have laughed along with her.

The tunnel didn't stray from its straight as an arrow path, just like the pixy had said. There had been the odd offshoot, but I'd ignored them. The dirt around us was solid, not too dusty, but more than that, the path seemed to be curving upward. There was no way that we were at the castle already. Not a chance.

I slowed my pace down to a trot and then full stop. "The tunnel is changing directions, it's climbing."

"You think she lied?" Lila asked quietly.

"No, I think something has changed."

Making myself lay down flat, I closed my eyes and pressed my ear to the ground. Lila slid off my back and crouched by my head. "You think Asag is pulling a fast one?"

"Yes." I breathed the word, a puff of dust curling up around my nose. That wasn't my focus though. The ground below us shivered and pulsed upward. I lifted my head, stood and found myself unable to be fully upright.

Well, that was not what we needed right then.

I almost said it out loud. The tunnel wasn't just changing directions, it was *shrinking*. Fuck me right up the pipe hole. "Lila, get on my back. Now."

I wasn't going to call attention to the fact that I'd realized the tunnel was shrinking around us. Not when we weren't near any way out that I could see. Maybe an offshoot was coming up?

Probably one that would pop us straight out into danger.

Goddess, damn it all to hell and back.

"Hang on," I muttered and forced my body back into a ground-covering, flat-out sprint. As the roof brushed the tips of my ears, I flattened my body out. That didn't last long, a few minutes, before Lila got scraped off.

"What the . . . is the tunnel—?"

"Yes." I didn't know if I had it in me to shift *again* even to my house cat form. I drew in a deep breath and tried to walk through that doorway in my mind. Nope, not a chance. The door was fucking locked.

"I can't . . . smaller." I scooted forward. Lila ran ahead of me as the space grew tighter and tighter.

I was belly crawling in a matter of minutes. Lila still had room.

Laughter boomed around us. "Concede defeat, Zamira of the desert." Asag's voice blasted through the tunnel, driving into my ears. "Give me my sister."

"Go," I yelled to Lila. "Go!"

"I'm not leaving you!" She yelled right back at me. "Keep moving."

I squeezed through the next ten feet, scrabbling and grabbing at the dirt to pull myself along.

"Here!" Lila screeched. "There's a way out!"

I followed her voice as the earth pressed in around me, pushing me down even as the soil below lifted up. One inch at a time I clawed my way toward her as the dirt rained down, blinding me.

Crushing. Suffocating. I gasped for breath. Lila dug her tiny claws into me and tried to help, I felt her pulling me along.

I closed my eyes and looked at the doorway in my mind. There was no other option, I had to shift.

The doorway was locked in my mind, so I threw myself at it, battering at it mentally. Lila was snarling and growling, I couldn't breathe.

I pressed with all I had against the doorway within me, kicking and screaming. It opened a crack. I forced myself through and with it my body had finally had enough.

Pain exploded in every part of me, as though every bone was breaking at once, and then there was nothing but complete and utter darkness and the knowledge that I'd failed everyone I loved.

I came to slowly, like I had been stuck in mud and left to bake in the sun. "Desert pie," I mumbled.

"Zam, Zam, talk to me." Lila tugged on my ears, yanking my head up. There was no light, we were in complete darkness. Maybe I'd died after all?

I couldn't feel anything, and after the pain that had erupted through my body, I wasn't going to complain about that. But my muscles were sloppy at best.

"I'm alive, I think," I said. "Where are we?"

"It's one of the offshoot tunnels," Lila whispered. "The other tunnel collapsed completely, and then Asag was howling with laughter, saying that he won. I heard him tell his demons to come and get Lilith for him."

I lay there, Lila holding my head tight. My tail twitched. Sure, I'd managed to shift into my house cat form, and stay alive, but at what cost? How long would it take for me to catch my wind? What would happen to Reyhan and Fen while we got our shit together?

"He thinks he killed us," I said softly.

"Yeah, I think he does. We've been here in this spot for over an hour, and nothing has come at us. Not one thing." She breathed out a heavy sigh. "It's good. We need to rest. But it won't last. Not if he's sending the demons to get Lilith."

Even though I'd just come to, I knew she was right. "Sleep for a bit, then we'll go."

Lila curled around me. "I wish we had some țuică."

I smiled, but even that felt difficult. "Me too."

Sleep was only at the edge of my body, so it was nothing to pass out again. This time I dreamed and knew I was in the dreamscape.

The Emperor, my grandfather, waited for me.

"Old bastard," I greeted him appropriately for his role in my life.

"Zamira, finding trouble still?" He raised his white eyebrows up nearly to his hairline.

"What are you doing here?" I didn't need to acknowledge that yes, I was in trouble. We all knew that was a key gift of mine.

"I don't know. I assumed you called me?" We stood next to a building that seemed to be within the demon city. There were no monsters here.

"Can you help me?" I asked. "Is there anything more about Asag that will help me defeat him?"

My grandfather closed his eyes and tipped his head back and forth as though he were trying to loosen up his thoughts. "He cannot be killed. Demons can't be killed, not by mortal means. They can kill one another. So your only hope is to banish him or bind him within an item." He shook his head. "Not that we need more cursed items in this world. The thirteen that there are, are plenty."

"What about a weapon like the flail, would that work?" I asked, choosing to ignore the comment about thirteen cursed items. I didn't need to borrow trouble, I had enough of my own.

He looked at me, eyebrows draw in tight. "You mean the sword you carry? Yes, that in theory could destroy a demon's essence. A lesser demon for sure; I do not know if even that sword would be enough to end Asag." He looked down at me. "The palace is closer than you realize now. You've come a long way."

He was right. "Asag thinks he killed me in that tunnel."

"Use it to your advantage. Stay small, slink through the darkness. You have other demons watching you, but I don't think that they will tattle on your progress. Those two want you to succeed."

I frowned. "Nico and Soleil."

"One of them for sure, and another that I can't quite see." He frowned too. "They have a vested interest in you succeeding. But by the rules, they can only help so much."

I stared out across what remained of the city. The wide swath that ran down the middle glittered with a barrier that kept everything out, just like the spells that Ishtar had used to keep me in the compound all those months ago. I sighed. That had seemed so terrible at the time, and now what I wouldn't give to be dealing with Ish again.

"So even if I lopped the fucker's head off, he could come back again. Somewhere else." I repeated his words back to him. To be sure.

"Yes."

"Flouncing satyrs," I muttered under my breath. "How do I banish him completely then? Do you know?"

He was quiet long enough that I turned away from the view of the city to look at him. "Do you know?"

"No." And with that, the asshat disappeared from the dreamscape.

Sighing, I sat myself down and looked out over the city. There was steam and light coming up from around the castle, as though there were a moat of warm water. "Probably lava," I snorted to myself. Just to make it interesting.

I needed restful sleep, so I pulled myself away from the dreamscape and sunk deeply into a proper sleep. Truly proper. Because I couldn't save anyone, couldn't stop any demon if I was dead on my feet.

A SOFT SHAKING of my shoulders woke me up. Then Lila's voice in the darkness. "Zam. We've been out for hours. We need to eat and move."

I lifted my head and swiveled my ears. There were no sounds in the dark of the tunnel, so that was good, and the soil below us was not moving. Also good. "I can't get to my pack."

All my gear, clothing, boots, and weapons shifted into a collar on my neck, holding it for me. So that I didn't have to do the naked shifting other shifters did. Which meant until I could step through the doorway in my mind back to two legs, we were shit out of luck for food.

"Come on, this way." Lila scuffled in the dark and I followed her, keeping my head close to her hip.

"I can't believe he thinks we're dead," I muttered. "Not that it doesn't work in our favor."

"Ego," Lila said. "Just like my father. He thinks he's indestructible. Which is part of his weakness. He's waiting on the army and the unicorns to sweep in and try to kill him. Probably has a trap for that too."

I snorted. "How many times have we been underestimated because of our size?"

"Every time," she whispered. "Zam, do you think we'll be able to get our powers back that he stole?"

Her words caused a slow tingle in my paw, where the bit of magic resided in me, left over from freeing it. "I have to believe we will, Lila. I think . . . maybe we need to snag our powers back first if we can. Slip into the castle, find where he's locked them away and then face him."

To be fair, I'd be happy to have my ability to heal and nothing else. That was a treasure beyond words. And I knew that Lila just wanted to be able to have her size back when she wanted to.

"Light is changing," she whispered.

I noticed the difference too. "Go careful."

We both crouched and slunk forward on our bellies through the tunnel, even though there was plenty of room for our tiny frames.

The light came from around the rectangular edges of a slab of brick that blocked the tunnel. Bits of ash and the smell of charred wood fluttered up my nose. "Another fireplace. In another house."

Which meant there had to be a trigger or something to open up the space. Right?

I put my paws on the backs of the bricks, pressing, looking for something that would give.

Nothing.

Christ on a crippled donkey, I could not wait to get through this challenge and be done with all the games.

Lila pushed me backward. "I got this." And promptly spit up acid all over the back of the bricks.

The sizzling and crackling of stone being disintegrated was music to my ears, even as I danced backward, away from a few droplets of the wicked acid. "Brilliant. Now let's hope that we don't need more of that any time soon."

"I didn't use much." Lila stepped out into the gloomy room first. It was still 'night' by the way the light reflected—or lack of light—reflected through the windows. "I'll be good if I need to spit my way through something else."

I padded around the edge of the room. This was the first moment that we'd truly been able to take a breath since we left the room in the inn. Even then, we'd been on the clock.

"Think you can shift?" she asked me quietly.

I stopped near a chair and closed my eyes, feeling my way to the doorway in my mind that would take me back to two legs.

The pain was instant, and shockingly bad. I fell

over, writhing as though a seizure had taken hold of me. Panting, I lay on the floor, unable to do anything but wait for the lightning bolts of agony to subside.

I was well and truly fucked now.

TWELVE

The big scorpion monster dragged us all the way across the desert but under the sand. Then we'd popped up, ran over a bridge and now into a castle.

He hadn't hurt us, but I was not happy that he'd taken me in the first place.

"It will be okay, Reyhan," Fen whispered in my ear. "I'll help you get away, then we will go find Lila and Zam."

I wrinkled up my nose at the smell of something stinky and awful that was all around us as we passed over the bridge. "I know. We'll be fine." Even though I felt dumb for putting the magic necklace on. I should have listened to Zam. But as we bobbled along with the giant scorpion man, I wasn't worried. I wasn't even really all that afraid.

At least it wasn't the rabisu.

"I am afraid I must leave you here, little one." The scorpion man dropped me to the floor of the castle as the massive doors closed behind him. He towered over me, looking down. His dark eyes said that he was sad and that he wasn't going to hurt me. I knew that. Even though he was large and terrifying to look at, he wasn't a bad man. "Hide if you can, little one. Fast as you can."

That was a good idea. I shifted quickly into my jungle cat cub shape and bolted deeper into the castle, Fen running alongside me. The floors were stone and carpet, and there were steps leading up into a small sitting space with plush chairs, thick pillows and even a blanket draped over the side of one arm.

A woman sat reading in one of the chairs, frozen. I paused, but she was just a statue. Good.

I leapt into the chair next to her and tucked under the blanket, laying as flat and still as I could in the hollow. Fen curled next to me. "Quiet."

I knew how to be quiet. That was what kept me alive so long in the rabisu's jungle. I turned up my lips at Fen, but didn't make a sound as the heavy boots stomped into the main room.

"Steven. Where is my newest pet?"

Oh, I didn't like that voice. It crawled over me, and dug under my skin like sand fleas. As much as I wanted to sink further down, I didn't dare move a single muscle.

"The one I brought escaped me the moment I stepped through the doors," Steven said. Steven the scorpion. That was silly. I smiled to myself, then the other one spoke and my smile was gone.

"Escaped you? I think not." I couldn't see the new voice, but I knew *he* was the bad guy. The bad one that Zam was trying to stop. Maybe my dad had been trying to stop him too?

There was a massive boom of thunder, only the thunder was more like the sound of cloth tearing, just very loud. I couldn't put my paws on the sound exactly. Tearing something, something wet. Something . . . screaming.

Steven was screaming and Fen carefully put a front foot over my head and covered my eyes. But that didn't stop the sounds from coming, over and over. I didn't need Fen to cover my eyes. I didn't want to see Steven get hurt. He'd told me funny stories all the way here. Jokes to make me laugh. Things to make me not be afraid. And then he'd tried to help me. He had helped me by telling me to hide.

The screaming cut off with a particularly loud sound of that wet, thunderous tearing. The smell of blood reached us, and my nose wrinkled in response.

"There. That was satisfying. But not as satisfying as the girl will be."

The footsteps were louder than I thought possible. He must be a giant of a man, huge, heavy, like a bull. Especially to have hurt Steven like that.

Those heavy footsteps circled around the main room and I held my breath a few times as they came closer.

"Tamisa, what did you see?"

"I saw nothing, boss. You took my eyes, remember?" The woman's voice was soft and gentle and I was horrified. She was no statue. She was alive! And if she'd heard us she could tattle on me and Fen.

"Bah, that's right. They were tasty." The bootsteps faded, thumping deeper into the keep. "I will find her soon enough. This is my castle, after all. She cannot hide forever. And then I will make her mine."

Fen shuddered and I didn't know why, I only knew that I didn't want to belong to a demon.

"It is safe for the moment," the kind, sightless woman said. Tamisa. I poked my head out from under the blanket. "He does not know you have two forms."

She hadn't moved from her position of holding a book, head bowed, eyes closed. Only they weren't closed, they were sewn shut. Her lips barely moved. "I am tied to this seat with his magic," she said without being asked. "There is a way to escape. But if he captures you, then there will be hell to pay."

"There is going to be hell to pay if he captures her at any point," Fen said. "Any help is appreciated."

"My left shoe," Tamisa whispered. "There is a key in it. My room on the fifteenth floor is as safe as you can be while you find a way to escape."

"That's a long way." Fen slithered out from under

the blanket and went to her left foot, and there was a key inside.

"Put the shoe back on," I said. "Or he'll notice."

"Good, you have sense in your head," Tamisa breathed out. "In my room is the key to banishing him. I almost had it. Take it with you, get to the Storm Queen."

I drew in a breath and her scent came to me. "You smell like the Storm Queen."

"She is my sister," Tamisa breathed. "I came to stop Asag. She said she would come with help."

"She's a right bitch," Fen whispered.

"Agreed," Tamisa said softly. "Go. The way to end him is in my room. You must get it to a Jinn woman. That will be his banishment. If my sister wasn't such a fucking twat, she could have done it."

"She's no lady," I said. "But I like you. Even if you say fuck."

"Go, little one. I will pray to the ocean goddess for your safety."

I wasn't sure that would help, seeing as her ocean goddess had obviously failed her, but I doubted she'd want a little girl pointing that out. I also wondered at how she'd known I had two forms? Maybe she could smell me too.

Fen wrapped the key up in his long, thin tail. "Rey-han, we go now. Hurry."

I scuttled out from under the blanket and stuck

close to Fen's side as we crept out of the reading area, and back to the main hall. There was no sign of Steven, except for the splashes of blue-green liquid on the floors and walls.

"Blood." Fen wrapped a wing over my back and tugged me along faster when I found myself slowing to look. "We have to move as quick as we can."

Scooting forward, we ran through the main entrance way to a narrower passage. There was only one way out of the big room which didn't leave us any choice. I sniffed the air, and Fen did the same.

"Stinks." My nose wrinkled, and I sneezed.

"Like shit," Fen whispered back.

But since that was the way out, off we went. I led the way and Fen kept close behind. Counting the steps, I took us all the way to the fifteenth floor, up the curving staircase. I wondered why there was just one narrow staircase here. Maybe there were others? What if there were a lot of people all at once that had to go up or down the stairs? What then?

The scent of poop faded, and was replaced with a different kind of horror for my sensitive nose. This one I knew all too well, even though I was just little. Blood. Lots and lots of blood.

I froze and the fur along my back and down my tail puffed up, giving me a little bit of height. Not a lot, but something.

Peeking out of the curving dark staircase, I took in

the hall in front of me. The floor was stone, but different colors, red, blue, green, yellow, black and even a few white stones. Big colors, big stones. I frowned.

It looked like a gameboard.

Fen peered out around me. "Looks like a trap." He leapt up, his wings beating the air and scooped me with his claws. "Safer this way."

I wrapped my front paws around his hold on me and clung to him. Because the feeling and smells that had set my fur to standing on edge had not eased off.

"Hurry," I whispered.

Fen grunted and flew forward, slow at first as we got going, and that almost did us in.

"I hear you," a voice called from the stairwell.

I bit down on the cry that nearly escaped my mouth. If I cried out, the bad man would have us for sure.

Fen flew faster. I clung to the key and the checked the doors. The last on the left, wasn't that what Tamisa had said? In my fear, I couldn't remember.

Fen dropped us down next to one of the doors and pressed us up against the wood hard. "Don't touch the stones. Shift, get the door open." Even though he was being so quiet, the laughter and voice from the stairwell heard him.

The demon heard him.

"Little kitten, you will be mine, oh how sweet!"

I shifted quickly and, shaking, jammed the key into the lock, turning it hard. It stuck.

No, this . . . couldn't be. I tried again, turning the key, but it wasn't working. It had to be the wrong door.

Fen growled and climbed up to my shoulder. "Stay close to the wall, scoot to the next one." His voice was calm even though I could feel him shaking. Or maybe it was me shaking.

I slid down the wall, my back pressed to the rough stone wall, the tips of my boots just touching the colorful steps in the middle of the hall. One of them depressed—a blue stone—and a matching blue mist shot into the air.

"Hold your breath and hurry," Fen said as he gulped in his own breath.

I closed my mouth and scurried faster until the next door was behind me. This was the last door on the left. The one I thought it should have been.

If it wasn't, we were in trouble. I jammed the key into the lock even as my lungs began to ache and the urge to breathe climbed through me. My hands fumbled and the click of the lock didn't compute at first.

Fen leapt from my shoulder and landed on the lever handle of the door, opening it so I stumbled through.

I fell to my knees and Fen shut the door carefully behind us, flew up and turned the lock.

He fell to the floor next to me and put his one claw to his mouth. Quiet. I could do that.

I lay there with my cheek pressed to the soft pink

carpet, keeping my breathing as slow and even as I could considering I'd just been holding my breath as we'd run.

I couldn't hear anything, but there on the floor I could feel the heavy thumps of the demon's boots going up and down the hall several times.

Was he yelling? Talking? Did he hesitate close to the door? I covered my ears with my hands and thought about my mother's lullaby to me.

You are my sunshine, my ray of sunshine
You make me happy when the desert dries.
You'll never know dear one, how much I love you
Even when, my heart breaks and cries.

"He's gone." Fen touched his nose to mine, and I opened my eyes. "It will be okay, Reyhan."

"How do you know that?" I whispered. Maybe I was more afraid than I realized.

The green-scaled, white-maned dragon let out a little puff of air. "I just do. We are alive. As long as we are alive there is a chance. Now we are on the inside. We will do what we can to help Lila and Zam and Maks to stop Asag. That is our task now. Tamisa gave us a task that could help."

Slowly I pushed up off my belly. I took a few breaths and then slowly sat up. "I'm hungry. Do you think there is anything in here to eat?"

Fen leapt up and wrapped himself around my neck. He was a little heavy. But I was glad for him, it felt like a hug. "We can look. But we will need to be careful, we don't know what might wait for us here."

I finally took a good look around the room. There was a simple bed on the floor, made up of stacks of blankets and pillows all in shades of red and pink. The rest of the floor was covered with a variety of rugs, all with different patterns. They overlapped one another on every edge.

To the one side of me there was an alcove and in the alcove was a table with old fruit on it. There were a few flies buzzing around the fruit. "Maybe there are nuts," I said.

Fen lifted his head. "Looks like some. And a jug of water. Probably stale, but it's better than nothing."

I stepped carefully across the rugs, flinching every time something moved under my foot. Was it a bug? Or something worse like a booby trap?

The table was a little bit too tall, so I climbed up and sat on the top while I shelled the nuts and popped them into my mouth. A little stale, but they weren't rotten. "You want one?"

Fen opened his mouth and I tossed him a nut that he cracked, spit out the shell and ate the flesh. We ate a bunch of nuts, then I grabbed the jug and lifted it to my mouth before checking.

The sour, sweet taste was like a punch in the mouth. "Tastes like plum." I hiccupped before I slid sideways, flat on the table top.

"Shit, I think you just got some alcohol, kid," Fen said, but his voice was distant and all I could think about was how warm and safe I felt as I drifted off to sleep.

CHAPTER

THIRTEEN

ZAMIRA

The pain from trying to shift when my body was so obviously done with all the back and forth took far longer than I would have thought to ease off. The minutes ticked by and my vision was fuzzy to the point that the world kept coming in and out of focus.

The house we'd sought shelter in smelled like all the others here in the demon city. Dusty, old, faint hints of demon. But it was safe—for the moment.

Lila's voice was right in my ear. "Zam, talk to me."

"Hurts," I whispered. That was the only word I could manage as my vision darkened around the edges. I kept breathing slowly, kept as still as I could, and the pain did ease off. But I hadn't shifted to two legs. I was still in my house cat form.

I don't know how long it was before I finally lifted my head. I felt like I'd been sick, like cotton had been stuffed between my ears and I'd been yanked through a knothole backwards. All at once.

"Nothing has come by," Lila said. "I think Asag doesn't know we are here."

"Good." I pushed slowly to my feet. Lilith was blessedly quiet. That could mean she was currently happy with the fact that I was stuck as a house cat, or that she hadn't figured out if it worked in her favor or not.

I decided to pull her in on the conversation. "Lilith, how could he not know we are alive? He said he sees everything. He wants us to bring you to him."

No demons have seen you since you were in the collapsed tunnel. That's how he watches you, through their eyes. And he will send them to find you. That you can be sure of.

That was surprisingly helpful. I passed on the information to Lila.

"So, the question is, how do we keep from any of them seeing us? The demons are damn well every-where. Obviously, since he knew exactly where we were." Lila shuddered and curled her tail around her front legs.

I tapped one paw on the floor, thinking. Thinking at least didn't make my bones feel as though they were being shattered from the inside out. But with that, I also did *not* want to think about what would happen if we made it all the way to Asag and I couldn't shift.

How the hell did I fight him then?

Warmth tickled along the top of my paw and I looked down. My black fur was as solidly dark as ever, however there was a slight . . . glow to the tips. Just on my paw.

Just where that tiny droplet of magic had decided to reside after I'd set it free.

I swallowed hard. "What if we could cloak ourselves, that would work, right? If he couldn't see us?"

Lila tapped me on the head gently. "You feeling okay? That's what we just said, that we need a way to keep him from seeing us. But how?"

Flexing my paw, I felt for the magic, trying to understand just how it would work. Because it was not my magic. Basically I knew from experience that using magic that was not your own could have deadly consequences; at the very least there would be a cost. Not unlike shifting.

I worried at my bottom lip. My belly growled, and I ignored the pain in my guts. Hunger was something we'd all lived with for enough time that it didn't bother me like it once had. "The magic," I whispered to Lila, feeling like at any point those instabilismori demons would poke their heads through the windows like damn rodents, "it's still in me. That tiny droplet. What if I could manipulate it somehow? What if I could use it to our benefit?"

Lilith shrieked inside my head, catching me off guard. I dropped to the floor and clamped my paws over my ears in an instinctive reflex. "Shut the fuck up, Lilith!" I growled.

How do you have magic? How did I not feel it?

"Because you aren't in charge," I snapped. "You don't rule, despite what you think."

Maybe that wasn't the best moment to point out that she wasn't as strong as she thought. We still needed her help. I still needed her to cut Asag's head off and banish him.

More than that, it gave her a reason to fight me again.

Lilith threw herself into taking over my body. I bared my teeth and lay still as the internal fight for control of my damn body raged.

Lila grabbed hold of me. "Kick her ass, Zam. You can do this, you did before." I tried not to hear the warble in her voice. The fear that Lilith would indeed win this round.

Greeting my teeth and letting out a low hiss, I used the last bit of my energy to wrestle Lilith away.

It took me only a minute to get her stuffed back into the corner of my mind, but I was exhausted. "Damn her. Damn you, Lilith!"

If she tried that when we were in the middle of a fight, I was going to get skewered. I couldn't fight on two sides of a battlefield.

"Okay, let's try this again," I muttered.

I flexed my paw that held the droplet of magic in it. Tried to feel my way around it. But it did nothing, didn't so much as give me a tickle of a response. "If you really want to help," I said, "you could fucking well give us a way to hide."

I waited, every sense on high alert. Nothing.

Damn it.

So now what? What was the point of having this magic if it was essentially a dead thing? Or maybe that's why it had stayed with me.

"Let's look at the facts," Lila said quietly. "There are two problems here. One is our size. The other is my body color. Even in the shadows, my scales glimmer and catch the subtle light. That will get us pinpointed in a flash."

The sound of sand moving outside the building froze me and my thoughts. I slunk to my belly and then scooted forward to hug the wall under a window. Lila leapt back through the hole in the fireplace and ducked down out of sight.

A murmuring of voices trickled through the open windows, all on top of one another.

"Fucking prick. I really hate him."

"We all do."

"But then why don't we kill him."

"Thems the rules."

"Stupid fucking rules."

"Yeah, yeah. Maybe find the cat and we helps her? Then we kills him."

"Then eats the cat?"

"Yeah, then we eats the cat."

Laughter followed their rather pointed back and forth.

Nico and Soleil had said that there would be some demons willing to help. In their own way. I looked over at where Lila lay hidden. "Gamble?"

"All at one cast," she muttered.

I took a breath and stepped out of the shadows. "Pity we can't find a demon who'd like Asag's crown. We'd help them if they helped us."

I pitched my voice low, just loud enough that it carried a small amount. A gamble indeed.

Then to Lila I mouthed, "*Henry IV.*"

She stomped a foot and then smiled. All at one cast indeed.

A head popped in with a hood up, but more than that, with his eyes closed. Smarter than the average demon then—Asag would not be pinpointing us with this one. "Cat?"

"Demon?" I tossed back. "If you can get us to the castle, we can kill Asag and put the crown on you."

Eyes still closed, the instablilismori demon flowed through the window, a shadow that had no strong form other than a vague human shape. The sensation of danger and evil that flowed with it made every bit of my fur stand on end.

"How can we trust you?" The demon circled around, eyes still closed. I flattened myself to the floor and took another chance.

All at one cast. "Nico and Soleil have helped us," I

said. "They want Asag off the throne and back into the realm of demons."

The shadow reeled back away from me a little. "Truth, I hear it in your words, cat. But I am not so sure that you can kill Asag. He's a beast."

"As am I," I said.

"Yous a cat." A second shadow flowed in, eyes closed on this one too.

"Yes, but I have other forms." I grimaced, knowing that they couldn't see me. "Stronger forms." Fuck, I hoped I still had other forms. I didn't want to think about the possibility that somehow I'd damaged my body enough that I wouldn't be able to shift anymore.

That would be the shits.

I pushed those thoughts away. "You get me to the castle, I'll put the crown on your head. I carry a weapon that will end Asag."

Inside of me, Lilith prowled, muttering under her breath.

"Why you help us be king here?" The first demon whispered his question. "What good would it do for you?"

I had to think quick on this one. "I don't care what demon rules, as long as it is not Asag. He has my . . . daughter."

The second demon slowed his circling. "Ahh, the little one. We did see her taken into the castle. Mother's revenge is strong. I know this."

I also realized that I was thinking of Reyhan like my

own child. Daughter it was then. If Jasten didn't survive Nico and Soleil, she was going to need someone to look after her.

"Deal then. We get you to castle, hidden in darkness. Unseen. You put crown on my head." The first demon crouched low, the shadows swirling around us.

They were dutifully keeping their eyes closed. That much was working so far.

"For me and my friend, hiding. There are two of you, and two of us," I said.

Lila popped out of her hiding spot.

"Who is your friend?" Their eyes were still closed. "The little dragon?"

"No. Another cat." I lied right to their faces. A gut feeling that if I said she was a dragon, the deal would be off.

"Done. Passage for two. Crown for us." The demons' darkness swirled and danced. "How do you want to hide?"

I looked him over. "Like this; if I stood under your feet, could you keep me hidden?"

"Bad idea, I don't want to be in a demon's skirts!" Lila hissed.

The demons turned to one another and they spoke back and forth, but their words were clicks and hisses.

Something about that was all wrong. Why?

My brain couldn't come up with the reason before they'd turned back to us. "Better that we take a form, and then carry you to the castle."

Their inky blackness that was their bodies began to solidify. Their eyes were still closed tight, keeping Asag out of things.

"Gotta be honest," I said. "You're going to look pretty fucking suspicious if you are solid and making a run for the castle with your eyes closed."

The darkness wavered. "What do you suggest?"

Was a demon really asking me what I thought? Yup, which was all the more reason to make my hackles dance. But what other choice did we have? None, that is the correct answer.

"Lila, step inside the shadows, let's see how well your . . .fur. . .stay hidden," I said. The last thing I wanted was to tip them off she wasn't a cat.

She glared at me. "I say I don't want to walk around inside a demon's skirts, and what do you say? You say get in the skirts."

Her grumbling continued as she hunched her shoulders and walked into the bottom of where the demon floated, stood, whatever you want to call it.

And she completely disappeared.

"Can you see?" I asked her.

"Everything is foggy, all black and white, but I can see," she said. "It's freaking colder than a witch's tit, Zam."

Cold we could handle. If we could see and stay covered, this was the way to go. Crazy as it seemed.

"That's how we'll do it. You two keep up to us." I bounded over to the other demon and landed inside the darkness. I could see out, just like Lila said. Black and white, the world was all stark contrasts now.

"If you run in a straight line, he will know," the demon with Lila said.

"So then the plan is, you two keep up to us," I said. Again. "We'll keep our patterns weird like you fools looking for us."

The demons both snorted in tandem but as I began to walk, my demon kept up with me. "You've attached yourself to us, that's it?" I asked. I'd had a shadow attached to me once, to track me. I didn't like it, but this felt similar.

"Yes." The demon surrounding me hissed the word. "Run as fast as you dare, you won't lose me."

I paused before I leapt up to the windowsill. "Lila, try . .. um .. .jump running." Yeah, not tipping off the demons was harder than I thought. Jump running.

Thank the goddess that Lila picked up what I was throwing down.

"Ooo, good idea! Jump running ha, that's a good one." There was the sound of her wings but there was no movement within the demon that I could see. "This is better, I won't tire as fast."

I took a deep breath. "Lila. If we get noticed, or draw attention, you take the left, I'll take the right. Meet at the castle."

"Wha . . . what?" She stuttered the word. "Split up?"

I bobbed my head, forgetting that she couldn't see

me, only knowing that I could feel my paw tingling along with my spidey senses that we needed to be ready. "Only if we have to—I don't want to—but just in case. Now let's go."

No more time needed to be wasted on guessing what might or might not happen.

I leapt up and out through the window and my dark shadow flowed with me. I scooted across the street and worked my way along the wall. I fully trusted that Lila would keep up. With no more thought about other demons, I shot into the house next to us, up the stairs and out the top window to the roof. From there I could clearly see what direction I needed to go, and I turned, leaping across the space between roofs.

Letting myself go in the moment, I turned on the speed and took off, feeling the shadow around me never waver. The buildings were stark in black and white and I took advantage of the clear view to keep making good time. We weren't far now from the castle, we were easily more than halfway.

I moved from rooftop to inside houses, down to the streets, along alley ways. Taking a left-hand turn, running past other demons, and dodging all manner of physical traps. They were clear as day now, vibrating with energy stored within them. Clever fuckers.

The dragons in cages were harder to ignore, but I kept my head down and tried not to hear their pitiful whimpers. Babies, they were babies and Asag was killing them.

But not for long, I had to believe we could save them.

Jaw tight, I focused on making my path erratic enough that no one watching us would notice. I slowed to a walk several times, and after a couple of hours, I ducked into a house.

The other demon followed, and I waited until he was inside and standing, or floating still, right next to me and my shadow.

"Lila, how are you holding up?" I asked. I couldn't see her. "Lila?"

A tremor ran down me and I reached for the bond between me and my friend. She was nowhere near me. Not even close.

Her energy was so far away that I bolted for the stairs that led all the way up to the third floor until I was sitting, teetering on the edge, and staring at the castle and right at where I could feel Lila was closing in.

Someone had snatched her, but how?

"Fucking demons!"

CHAPTER
FOURTEEN

I didn't even pause at the window ledge once I felt Lila's energy almost to Asag's castle. I leapt from the window, totally trusting that my shadow would stay with me.

Lilith laughed from inside my head.

Fool. Did you really think that a pair of shape-shifting demons could be trusted?

I didn't trust them! I threw my thoughts back at her. I was using them!

You could have just asked me, I could have hidden you away from the demons' eyes and gotten you all the way to Asag. But no, you would rather trust unknown demons. You would rather gamble your friend's life than to trust me.

I was running for all I had, and the shadow was keeping up. Without worrying about anyone else matching my pace, without wondering if Lila would be seen, or if Maks would get taken, I turned on the speed.

Drawing energy off my connection to my brother and the pride, I felt their eyes turn my way. I didn't want to use their strength, but they gave it freely, and I used it to fuel my limbs. I should have done it sooner, but I was loath to pull from them when I'd told them to go. To get to safety.

What will you do when you get to the moat of lava, fool? What will you do to make Asag drop the stone gate so that you can enter his castle? There is no other way! You needed your little dragon, and she was taken because you forgot to make her part of the deal!

Lilith wasn't even laughing at me. She was berating me, and I deserved it. I'd made the deal for two cats—not a cat and a dragon. The only thing I could do now was just lock onto the energy of Lila, Fen and Reyhan and pray to the desert gods that I could not only make it in time, but that I would still have something left to finish Asag off.

I reached for Maks' threads and found him behind me, and more to the east. Still within the city, but he wasn't hurt. He wasn't scared. Confusion and frustration came through loud and clear, but that was it. Maks hadn't been taken, and that was the only thing that kept me running straight for the castle.

How will you get him to lower the drawbridge and open the stone gate? Do you have a plan?

I didn't have a solid idea, but as I ran, one began to form. What did Asag want from me enough to give me more time to get to Reyhan and Fen? Not just entertainment.

He wanted Lilith.

"What will he give me, to keep you for himself?" I asked her. "The answer is anything."

He wants to kill me! Lilith shrieked. But again, under her seeming upset I could feel a tiny strand of glee. Enough to tell me that Lilith wanted badly to get to Asag, no matter how it happened.

I didn't slow my pace. In the black and white view of the world that I had, avoiding all the traps was easy.

Going unseen by other demons, super easy.

Lilith? I called her name, inside my head.

What?

There was a pile of lumber that I scrambled over, digging my claws in and leaving big divots in the wood. "I know I'm going to die. I fully don't expect to survive this."

She was quieter than she'd ever been before, listening to me.

"Make sure that you kill him good for me," I said.

You believe that I am capable of killing him?

"You told me you could kill demons. That only demons could harm other demons. If you can't kill him, who else is there?"

I leapt over another trap, not even bothering to look down. This was part of my plan, and I had to play it right or she would see right through it.

"I don't know how, but I think you had something

to do with us being thought of as dead in the tunnels," I said softly to her. Nope, I didn't believe it for a second, but I wanted her to think I did.

Snaking between the houses, I kept my pace on point. "And I think that you are helping me get to him, so that you can kill him, banish him, whatever it is that you think can be done. Just do it. I'll get you there. You finish him off."

The pause in her was heavy. *I will finish him. He will wish he'd never been thought into existence.*

I didn't want to push it any more, but I felt the shift in her.

When I tell you . . . you must turn on the speed even more. I will help the demon detach from you.

"I'll be seen."

She hummed with pleasure. *No, you won't. I guarantee that Asag will* never *see you coming.*

Goddamn it, why hadn't I taken this route before?

Not just because I didn't trust her, but because I knew that outsmarting a demon was no small thing.

And now I had to outsmart not one, but two. And they were siblings. Fuck my luck.

"Tell me when."

The demon around me didn't so much as respond to me seemingly talking to myself. I was running flat out down a street that currently was headed west. Away from the castle. But not all of them led straight to Asag. And so far, my ability to stay undetected was solid.

Shall we give Asag a scare? He will not expect his demons to turn on him. Nor will he expect you to be this close.

"Not if he is going to hurt my family," I said, but I could already feel the shadow around me being . . . pushed off was the only word I had for the sensation. Like it was being scraped away with a sword maybe, shaving me clean of the darkness.

He wants you to suffer, Zamira. He will wait to kill them until the moment is so sweetly painful, he won't be able to resist. Not until you are looking that little girl in the eyes will he cut her throat.

She said those words as if that option was better. Not that it mattered, because she was removing the shadow. I steeled myself for what was coming.

And just like that, the world was back to brilliant, wild color and I could *feel* those eyes on me again.

I turned and looked at the demon behind me, straight in the eyes, knowing that Asag could very well see me. "Surprise, motherfucker!"

Lilith crowed with laughter and then I took off. We were so much closer to the castle now, but we were hardly in the clear.

All around us, a bellow of rage boomed as Asag truly saw us, and every demon in the vicinity slunk down low. They were going to be in trouble, of that I had no doubt.

Your friends slow you down, cat. I think perhaps you even held back with the demon cloaking you.

I leaned into my run, flattening out and using every sense I had to avoid the traps—which seemed almost obvious now that I'd viewed them in black and white —and to avoid the demons.

The sand traps were simple now. Tiny grains of sand shivering were my tip-off and I scanned the ground constantly.

The demons were not as easy to avoid, but they almost seemed to be not looking at me. "What gives, Lilith?"

I have my own ability to cloak what I am, Zamira. I have slid that cloak over you. The eyes run off the edge of your body like water off the edge of a sword. It is partially why I lay hidden inside Mamitu's armory for so long. I did not wish to be picked up by an egotistical man who believed he could destroy Asag. Not when I knew I would sense the right one when she came. I just did not expect that you would be so strong.

I bounced off a sidewall, up onto a wooden barrel and then leapt right over the head of a demon. I was quiet until we were well past that demon—I was not going to test my luck, as shitty as it was being.

"You knew I had a chance?"

You had the best chance. I can see your ancestry, Zamira. All those powerful bloodlines converging into one body? Blood of a Jinn, witch, fairy, shifter, blood of the Emperor himself . . . there was no better opportunity for me to find my way back to Asag than within your hands.

Of course, she was chatty now, we were getting

close to our destination, and she thought I was just going hand myself over to her. I held nothing back on my speed, and just ran for all I was worth. I could feel the threads tying me to Lila, Reyhan and Fen. They weren't together exactly, but they were close. And no one was hurt.

Yet.

I'm surprised you are not feeling badly for the hatchlings. Trying to stop and save them. Do not mistake me, I am glad for your coldness.

We passed under a cage with a dragon limp inside of it. I spared it a glance but no more. "I can't save any of them if I can't stop Asag," I said simply. It wasn't that I didn't feel badly for them. I just knew that there was only one way this was going to work. With Asag locked away, or better yet, dead on the end of Lilith's point.

A demon shot out of a building right in front of me, only it wasn't a demon.

It was a demon taking the shape of what had to be my deadliest, most manipulative enemy.

Merlin.

I couldn't help it, I skidded to a stop, going sideways until I bounced into a wall.

His smile was wide as he stared down at me, looking straight through whatever magic Lilith had cloaked me with. "You didn't think you'd actually killed me, did you? That I, Merlin, a mage of my level could be killed by *you*? A mere shifter of the desert?" He snorted. "Please."

Damn it, he is stronger than the others! Lilith growled. *I will try again to hide you!*

"You aren't really Merlin." I moved to sidestep around him, but the middle of the street had that perfect shimmering vibration of a sand trap. Fuck. I went to leap up to the window and he caught me in mid-air, his fingers wrapped tight around my ribs.

How? He'd been ten feet away, and then bam! He was just there before I could even blink.

He squeezed as he smiled at me. "You didn't think you'd escape, did you? Or that you'd actually be able to defeat Asag? You're a nothing. You were a nothing in the west, and you are a nothing here in the east."

I flexed my paws and slashed at his wrist. With Lilith a part of me, my claws made a deep, violent gouge through skin and bone, forcing him to release me.

He screamed and dropped me. I turned to run, but there were demons behind me now too.

"Lilith." I snarled her name.

Never trust a demon.

I gritted my teeth, took a breath, and stepped sideways into the pit. "I didn't."

FIFTEEN

LILA

W hat the actual fuck was happening now? I was wrapped up in the darkness of the demon one second and looking at the world in black and white, and the next I couldn't see anything.

Nada.

Zip.

Bupkiss.

It took less than a split second to realize that Zam and I were being separated, duped by the demons. There was a weird sensation of being passed over, like the demon who we'd stupidly agreed to was handing me off to something else. Another demon?

Again. We'd been fooled *again*.

I fought and struggled to get out of the new demon's skirt. "I knew this was a bad idea!" I twisted around, trying to untangle myself from the demon, but it was an effort in futility. Stupid, stupid! We should have just kept on going on our own.

"Asag will reward me," the demon whispered. "Greatly. You are one of the keys. Three keys, three souls and he will be strong enough to break free of his cage."

Now that I did not like the sound of, but that didn't mean I wouldn't try to understand what was happening. If I could get information that would help us, I would. "Well, there is only me, so that is only one key, you fool of a tattered bedsheet!"

The demon snickered, the air pulsing around us. "He has the little one already. The girl, she is one of the souls he needs. The queen of the dragons is the second. And the third is—"

"Zamira, guardian of the desert," I offered. Of course it would be Zam. Why wouldn't it? She was the center of our family and always the center of trouble—

"The Jinn master," he breathed. "That one is needed too. Maybe I shouldn't be telling you this?"

Oh . . . son of a raging bitch. "Maks?"

"I don't know a Maks. I know a Roshawn. And Asag released Roshawn to go and find a new body, but Roshawn thinks he escaped. Thinks that he got away. Doesn't realize he is needed." Again that strange pulsing in and out which I suspected was laughter. "Asag made up all sorts of prophecies, and sent them out into the world. And those prophecies brought what he needs. That and a unicorn horn. I almost forgot. But he is smart this one, Asag is smart and I am going to be his best friend. And he has his whole family helping him!"

Oh . . . kay. I wasn't sure how to use all this information. Chatty Kathy here was spilling the tea, but I needed to figure out if I could make it work for me. "You want a friend? I can be your friend. I'm a great friend!"

"Yes, yes, Asag as a friend would be amazing." The demon sighed and its pace slowed. "You know that I was his friend once? And then I did something, I can't remember, and he stole a part of me. The thinking part, he said. Because the thinking part is the part that he didn't like. I think maybe . . . maybe I was the reason he is locked up in his castle."

Sweet, so I had the defector of all defectors, and . . . "Wait. His *whole* family is helping him?"

"Well, yes. If Asag is free, he can open the portal between earth and the demon realm. Then Nico and Lilith can both be with him. He loves Lilith, you know. Like looooooooves her." Another pulsing of air in and out, though a little slower this time. Maybe a giggle?

I thought about what Zam had said. That we had to gamble now to make it to the end of this. I drew in a shaky breath. "What if I could take you to Roshawn? Maybe then Asag would be my friend too?"

I had to be able to outsmart this demon.

The sensation of movement slowed. "You would do

that? To help me? I would like my thinking part back. Very much."

"If we're going to be friends, then yes. I would do that." Come on, take the bait, take the bait.

He slowed further. "You think Roshawn is close?"

"He's with my friend, Maks," I said, being careful with my words. "And they are here in the city too, but I can lead you to him. Then Asag could be my friend too." I didn't dare hold my breath for fear that it would tip the demon off. "Do you have a name?"

"I did at one time, but I don't now."

"Can I give you a nice name?"

The darkness swirled and I got a glimpse of buildings. "Maybe."

"If you go into one of those buildings. And close your eyes, and put me down, I'll give you a name and then we can go and find Roshawn." Suddenly I understood why Zam kept on trying to make things work with Lilith. Why she kept trying to make deals with demons. Because once you got backed into a corner, you had nothing to lose by making a deal with the devil.

I felt bad for giving her so much shit about it.

The building closest to us was more like a pile of rubble with a bit of a roof on it. "This work?"

"Yes, but no other demons can see me. Otherwise we can't make this a great surprise for Asag." I kept my voice low. Just in case there were others close.

"You going to give me a name now?" The swirling darkness seemed . . . intent on that.

"Put me down first," I said.

I was plunked onto the floor and the demon's inky shadows pulled away from me. Eyes closed, it crouched down low, pooling on the floor. "Better, friend?"

"Yup. Now, a good name. The name of a great friend, right?"

"Oh, the best of friends," he purred. Definitely a he.

"Male?" I asked, just in case I was wrong.

"Yes, I am male. So, you will give me the best of names? The name of a friend so great, Asag will know me just by my name?"

No pressure there. "Yes, let me think a moment, I want to be sure. Can you watch for any other demons? Make sure that they don't come around?"

"You bet." The demon slid away, up and out the window.

Shit, that was easier than I thought it would be to make him leave. I took a step to fly away, straight out the far window.

And if I did that? Another demon would be on me in a flash. My scales were far too colorful, too bright.

If I stayed . . . I would have to get Maks either way, and my new-ish friend might actually be able to help me do that.

I paced the room, thinking. If I took the demon's help,

and got to Maks, we could work together to . . . what, leave? If this demon was right, then Maks and I were part of the keys that Asag had been working to gather all along. We also needed to get to Zam and tell her that there was no bad blood between Lilith and Asag. That Nico and Soleil were not trying to send Asag back to the demon realms, but instead were trying to help him *open* them up.

That we'd been played all along . . . right from the satyr flouncing beginning of this journey.

"What to do, what to do?" My tail twitched and lashed as I tried to think through all the scenarios that could come from me taking one path or another.

Finally, I stopped in the middle of the room and closed my eyes. It had been a long time since I'd thought about my mother. She was gone, long dead. But I remembered everything she'd ever told me, little as it might have been.

Hearts don't lie.

I swallowed hard. "Friend. I have a name for you. The best of names."

The demon all but blasted back in. "A name, a name for me! Thank you!"

"The name I am going to give you is very strong, and very brave, but also very loyal." Here's to hoping I could really lock this demon and his help down. "And I'm giving it to you, so you will be *my* friend."

"Yes, wonderful!" That fluttering of air that I suspected was laughter poured out of him.

"Why are you laughing?" I shrunk away from the darkness. Suddenly unsure of my decision.

"So happy, I have been nameless for so long. So long, and a new name, one that is so good will make things right." Again the demon pooled up on the rubble across the floor. Long, spindly arms and hands reached out to pull itself along. There was the shape of a head, eyes closed, but mostly it was just shadows.

"Robert," I said. "That's your name."

A shudder went through the demon, and the darkness solidified into the body of a man with dark hair to his shoulders. He sat in a crouch, head down, fists on the rubble holding him up. "You gave me a name, little one." His voice was deeper now; more than that, it was . . . solid.

Oh, shit.

"That unlocked something, didn't it? Giving you a name?" I whispered, cursing myself. "Fuck, giving you a name unlocked something!"

His laugh was soft and when he lifted his head, he looked right at me with the bluest of eyes. I backed away and he carefully held up a hand. "He cannot see you through my eyes now. And yes, you unlocked the curse he put on me, to keep me mute, to keep me complacent." Blue eyes, not the demonic red that I'd expected.

"Why can't he see me through you?" I found myself cringing against the wall as far from my newly named friend as I could get. Damn it, Asag would be on me in a flash, him and his horde of demons!

"Because I am only half demon. Asag and Lilith were born of Nico. I was born of Soleil. We're a . . . I believe you call it a blended family." He held a hand to me. "We need to find Roshawn. With his help, we can cast out Asag, once and for all—perhaps even kill him. Asag has brought his doom to his doorstep, without even realizing it."

I stayed where I was. "How do I know you aren't lying to me? Every single *fucking time* we start to trust someone, they turn on us."

Robert nodded. "Fair. I suppose I have no way to explain to you the hatred that is in my heart for Asag— he tried to rape my mother, and he destroyed my father. But Roshawn will speak for me. I was the last of the brethren to fall to Asag's power, and it was I with Roshawn's help who condemned him to his castle. It's why he uses other demons, to watch through their eyes. He is unable to leave."

"What about my friends in the castle?"

Robert's face went thoughtful. "He will hunt them, and when he finds them they will be his play toys for as long as he can keep them alive."

My heart plummeted for Reyhan and Fen. "So we have to hurry."

"That would be best." He paused. "But I do believe I have a way of showing you that I am trustworthy."

I flicked my tail, lashing it back and forth. "Yeah, how's that?"

Robert scooped up a piece of rubble, a chunk of rock about the size of my head, and tossed it out the window.

I tucked myself behind a pile of blasted up bricks. "You'll bring one of the other demons here!"

"Necessary, to prove myself to you," he said. "I need you to trust me, and we need to make it happen fast."

The air in the room cooled as a shadow figure slid in through the window. "What is this?" It let out a low hiss. "Who are you?"

Robert moved fast, closing the distance between them and wrapping his hand around the demon's neck area. "Asag."

The shadow figure danced and jigged like a fish on a line as its eyes went from red, to a deep burning orange as Asag took hold of the demon. "NO!" He bellowed. "This cannot be!"

Robert only tightened his grip. "You truly believed I would never come back? I will send you and your family back to the depths of the demon realms, Asag, if it is the last thing I do!" my new friend snarled. "And I'll start with your little friend here."

With his free hand, he drew a circle in the air and the space beside him opened. I watched as what could only be a portal unsealed the spaces between our world and somewhere else. That somewhere else being what I suspected was the demon realm.

With a flick of his hand, holding the demon around the neck, he threw it into the opening and then snapped his fingers, shutting it before it could scramble back out.

Robert turned to me. "Satisfied?"

Almost. "You know any Shakespeare?" This was my litmus test. If he knew Will, he was in.

Robert crouched down and held a hand to me. "Doubt thou the stars are fire; Doubt that the sun doth move; Doubt truth to be a liar; But never doubt I love."

I bobbed my head and leapt up to his shoulder. "*Hamlet* is acceptable, but not my favorite to be sure."

"More of a *Romeo and Juliet* are we?" He snapped his fingers again and a black cloak swirled up and around us. We weren't hidden the same way as the shadow demons, but we sure as hell weren't sticking out like sore thumbs.

I shook my head. "Let's go hand in hand, not one before the other."

His laugh was a low chuckle. "*Comedy of Errors.* Also an excellent choice."

A slow breath left me. If he knew Shakespeare that well, then it was meant to be. "Let's go find the boys."

CHAPTER

SIXTEEN

ZAM

H ere's the thing. Jumping down and into one of the sand pits was, indeed, a last-ditch effort not to get caught by Asag's demons. To escape another inescapable situation.

Because at the rate me and my friends were going, we were all going to get stuck in Asag's goddess-damned castle, and he'd win the world, we wouldn't free the dragons, and we'd all end up in a dungeon for what remained of our natural lives.

Unacceptable.

The leap down into the pit was supposed to go smoother than it actually did.

I landed on the thin reeds that ran across the pit in a crosshatch pattern. My legs were splayed out in all four directions as I balanced on the reeds. "For fuck's sake, I can't even drop into a pit without something going wrong!" I snarled. That being said . . . the demons on the left and behind me hadn't swung around to the far side of the pit. There was an opening for me to escape.

One leap, that was all I had. I knew from previous experience that the thin reeds wouldn't take anything more than that to buckle underneath me.

"Grab her!" The cry went up all around, from every shadow figure at one time.

"I think I preferred your golems, Asag!" I yelled as I pushed off. The reeds bent under me, and there was something snaking up from inside the pit. Maybe a sand snake, maybe the hand of a giant. I didn't stick around to see what it was.

The push-off didn't go as well as planned. Without the steadiness of ground beneath me, I kind of kicked off and fell, rather than leaping.

"Fuck!" I scrambled across the falling reeds, using every bit of cat dexterity I had in me until I was clinging to the edge of the pit, hanging from the tips of my claws, and realizing I'd somehow made it.

Maybe I did have a little bit of luck left to me then.

Pushing off with my back feet, I pulled myself up as the thing in the pit grabbed for the tip of my tail. I snapped my tail away and didn't look back as I ran straight for the drainpipe chains hanging off the house closest to me.

Up I went while the shapeshifting demons below me howled, their eyes all bright orange. Asag was really on me now. There was no way that I was going to be able to escape his eyes at this rate.

"Lilith?"

My ability to cloak you is not working! I don't know why!

Yeah, no shit it wasn't working, but I wasn't buying her 'I don't know why' business.

Demons. If I never had to deal with them again, I would die happy. They were all a bunch of fucking liars.

I crawled through the top window of the house and instead of running down the stairs in front of me, scooted across the room and leapt out the far window. I would use the rooftops as best I could now. Asag could see me with all those demons on my ass; I might as well bank on my speed.

A roar of anger bellowed suddenly through the open skies, so heavy and thick I felt it press down on me, physically slowing me down.

"I'll kill them all for your insolence!" Asag roared. "Your little friends will die!"

I tapped into Reyhan and Fen. No fear. Reyhan was sleeping, and Fen was alert but no I'm-about-to-die-at-the-hands-of-a-demon kind of fear. I locked hard onto those threads and kept running. It was all I could do.

Lila . . . was behind me? And close to Maks? That was good if they were together, she must have gotten free of the demon. I trusted that they would get to me.

The buildings blurred in the ever-existing night, the shadow figures leaping out distorted the world, but my goal was the only thing that mattered.

I was running out of time. I had to get to them. I had to trust that I could make it in time.

What I didn't expect was for Asag to suddenly pull the rug out from under me. In the most literal of senses.

I could see the castle clearly, could see the bubbling of what could only be lava ringing around the base of the castle.

Lava. Fuck, I'd half hoped that Lilith was just trying to freak me out.

"I'm coming for you, motherfucker," I snarled. I'd figure out the lava somehow.

The sound of wings tipped my ears as I ran. Wings could be anything, but I was betting nothing good.

There was a feeling of pressure around me, and I dropped flat to the rooftop I was on, sliding sideways as I dug my claws in, scrabbling to keep from sliding right off the edge.

The wings that went over me were feathery. I looked up, half hoping that my rhuk friend, Cassandra, was back to save the day.

No rhuk.

This was something—someone—else entirely.

"Soleil," I breathed out her name.

She swooped down, landing on the peak of the roof in front of me. "You are the only one who can see me.

You must trust me. There are far more threads than you could ever imagine tied into this game that Asag is playing. His father and sister are working with him. Despite what they say."

Liar, she's a fucking liar! That cunt would say anything to throw my brother back into the demon realm!

Lilith felt her slip-up right when I did. Goddess-damned demons!

"What do I need to do?" I asked.

Soleil landed and her body went translucent, like an overlay on the world. "Go back to the beginning. Asag needs the horn of your friend to complete the spell that would free him from the castle. He will open the gates for you, though it will look like he made you fight for it. Use Lilith against the demons. She will hate it, she will fight you, but every blow she deals truly sends another demon back to the realm."

"Why now? Why not tell me sooner?" I yelled at her, even as I felt the shadows creeping closer. I realized that her presence was what was keeping them at bay. "All this way! Almost dying in the tunnels and you want me to go BACK?"

I couldn't believe it. If we'd just fucking waited, he would have opened the gates and let us in?

"He would not have opened the gates sooner. He wants to make you suffer, and suffer you have," she said, not reading my mind—my damn jaw was hanging open. "But he has the child somewhere in his keep, and he is actively hunting for the last Jinn master. Without that horn, he cannot complete his task."

My guts twisted up and my heart plummeted. "Maks."

"You must not go for him. I have done what I can to put a helper in place to keep him safe. But for Asag to leave the castle, he needs three things. And the Jinn master, your unicorn's horn, and the child are those three things."

If I thought my guts were knotted up before, it was nothing to what I felt right then. "And all the prophecies, they were just . . ."

Her eyes were sad. "Just the pieces of a game to him —lies to bring the right things to him when he needed them. Mamitu and Pazuzu were never your friends. *Never.* Mamitu is not dead, Zamira." She looked over her shoulder and her face twisted up in pain. "I have . . . Nico is coming. I must go."

I grabbed at her, clawing at her ankle, or at least trying too. My claws went right through her ghostly form. "Into the house. You're going to tell me everything you can."

Her shoulders and wings slumped, but she slid into the house after me, curling around herself to fit through the open window.

"Explain." I growled the word. "Quickly."

Soleil crouched down so we were closer. "Nico has two children. I have one child. We were a family for a little while. I thought . . . I thought I had changed

Nico." She shook her head and waved a hand through the air. "He believes I am helping him, and that I do not realize that his goals are not mine. He would set Lilith and Asag on the throne here together. Together, they would be unstoppable, Zamira. Together they would topple the world."

I locked my front legs to keep from wobbling.

She went on. "Asag has been spreading false prophecies for years, trying to get people to reach him with the correct pieces of the puzzle. He has been stealing young girls for the same reason, looking for the right one. Looking for the one that has the blood-lines he needs."

"Why make it so fucking hard then? I am the first to get through!" I snapped the words, anger and fear making me sharp. Okay, I was always sharp, but sharper than my normal.

She grimaced and even that was beautiful on her face. "Because there is still balance, and there are still rules that must be followed. There is a cost, Zamira. A cost to him being here in this world. A cost to him wanting to take over. Mamitu and Pazuzu helped every single soul that has ever tried to come after Asag. Guided them. They lied to you. You are not the first to get this far. You aren't even the one hundredth. But none came with the things Asag needed."

Her eyes were locked onto mine and I could see the sadness in her. "Then why would you help me *now*?

Why tell me to go get him the fucking horn?" I was backing away from her.

Games, they were all playing games with me, and I couldn't see the board or the rules myself.

"Because you are the first that *I* have helped," she whispered. "You are the first who has actually come with the things he needs to free himself. Because those same things needed to free him, are also what is needed to cast him back into the demon realm. Do you see? Balance." She crouched even closer and lowered her voice. "There are no prophecies, Zamira of the desert. There is only the strength of your heart and conviction to save those you love. The child. The horn. The Jinn master. The lines spoken as Asag is removed of his head."

Lilith was suspiciously quiet. Was it because Soleil was telling me the truth?

"I carry Lilith," I said softly.

"I know. She is more dangerous than Asag, but together . . . they would be monstrous. Watch her. She is waiting for her moment to strike; she is like a venomous snake."

Watch her.

As if I didn't already.

Soleil's eyes fluttered, her long lashes brushing across her cheeks. "I do not have much strength in this world, Zamira. I would need a body, and I am loath to take one as Nico has taken your friend Jasten."

"You weren't in him?"

She bobbed her head. "For a time I was so that Nico would trust me. I left, so as to give the body a better chance at survival. Nico is searching now for a stronger body. He left Jasten out in the city."

I shuddered as my thoughts ramped up. Was she asking for a ride? "I already share my body with Lilith."

"I know. You must go, they will find us soon." She stood. "I will try to lead them off you. Get to your horse, the horn is with him."

Crazy, I was fucking crazy for even thinking this. Because the horn was not with Balder.

The horn was already with me.

"Soleil. Come with me. I will carry you. I can . . . carry you both."

What the actual fuck do you think you're doing? I am not going to share space with my twinkie blasted step-mother, just because you think she's telling you the truth!

The thing was, Lilith was well known enough to me that I *knew* when she was lying and when she was telling the truth. I also knew when she was trying to manipulate me.

Her energy was fucking through the roof, terrified.

Soleil put a hand out to me, but she did not touch me. "You cannot. It is enough that you contain Lilith without breaking. Though I suggest you shift soon so that she is not so much a part of you."

I shrugged my little shoulders. "Blocked. Something is blocking me, too many shifts. Which means that Lilith is pretty much fucked."

Her scream resonated through me and Soleil lifted her brows. "She was always angry about something. I see that has not changed."

"Welcome to my world," I said.

Soleil spread her wings and the light around us changed. "It cannot always be night." Her eyes glowed a brilliant blue. "Run. I will scatter them for you."

"It's too far to the gate," I said. "It will take me too long."

Trusting her was not something I took lightly. But for that moment, I felt a connection to Soleil.

"Then I will help you with that." Her eyes closed and I felt something pick me up, something that I could not see. If I closed my eyes, it felt like feathers were cupped around my body, but I didn't dare close them for long.

Without another word between us I was flung south, faster than the unicorns or Balder could move. The speed stole my breath.

I blinked and was dropped into a house more than halfway back to the gates. All the ground covered, lost.

Good thing I had a plan, right? Yeah, right.

With nothing for it but to keep moving, I took off, running south. Out the window, and flying through the air to the next house. How many days had I run toward Asag's castle, and now I would go the other direction? But they would not be looking for me.

Not going south. Not with Soleil giving me a head start like that.

Did I need the horn? No, I already had it. But if I could get to Balder, then gather up Maks and Lila . . . we would face Asag together.

Lilith screamed inside of me, thrashing about.

No! You wanted me to kill Asag, we are going the wrong way!

I had no doubt about that. She'd wanted me to get to her brother so they could topple the world. Fools, we were all fools!

Behind me a brilliant flash lit up the sky and a cacophony of shrieking, glass-shattering screams rent the air, sending every hair on my fur-covered ass to try and leave my body.

I'd never been so puffed up—ever. Not that it slowed me.

But already I had a plan forming. Something that I tucked away from Lilith so she would not spoil it. A plan that might, just might have Asag begging for mercy.

The sky above was as bright as if it had been painted a brilliant white, and I realized as I ran, straight down the sandy streets, that was what Soleil had done. She'd lit up the clouds somehow.

I reached out for my connection to Bryce. He was south and I felt my brother turn my way.

I sent him the image of what I wanted and followed it up with words.

"Let Balder come to me."

SEVENTEEN

Robert was fast for having only two legs. And no wings. And for being some version of a demon. I wondered if he cared that I'd named him Robert. Surely that was not his real name.

I clung hard to the back and side of his neck with my claws and he didn't make a peep.

I kept my sense locked on Maks. "Further east, a little north," I muttered.

The half-demon didn't slow, and he didn't question my directions. I'd give him that, he was a rather quiet type. Not overly chatty. Then again, he was running flat out and not given to having a lot of air left to speak was my guess.

My bigger concern was *me* second guessing myself. Sure, Robert had sent some instabilismori demon off to la-la land. But demons weren't above killing or banishing one another. One only had to look as far as

Lilith to see that truth. She was happy to cut through other demons without any concern . . .

"If Zam can use Lilith on Asag, could that send him back to the demon realm?"

Robert put a hand on a downed barrel and hopped over it. "In theory, yes, but I'd bet that she would fight being used on him. She knows her capabilities and I worry that if she is used on him, that she will have something up her sleeve. It will be best to have the spell ready."

In theory.

Hmm.

"You haven't run into many traps," I pointed out as we ran cleanly down another main street.

"They aren't setting the traps for me. They are setting them for Zamira."

"I thought Asag didn't need Zam?" I frowned and found myself digging in tighter on a matter of principle. I didn't need him lying. And I could feel his heart rate change by holding a little tighter.

He grunted. "He doesn't. But who will come to her rescue?"

"Her brother and all the unicorns." I groaned as I spoke because I realized the real trap laid out. "We have been played so damn hard! This is the shits, you know that?"

"Demons are master manipulators, little one. Do not feel bad. I fell for their lies too." He actually sounded sad. "I believed . . . that Asag was the brother I had always wanted. That Lilith was my friend. But they used me, as they used my mother. We were," he paused at the edge of a house and peered around the side. "Just tools to them. Just as you and your friends are tools to them."

My jaw ticked. Sadness rolled off around him.

I sighed. "Well, then we're all in the same damn bucket."

He slipped around the corner and then picked up speed. "Are we closing in?"

I tuned into Maks and gave a yip. "There! He's just off to your right!"

I let go of Robert, pushed off and flew hard. He reached for me and managed to grab my tail. I turned around hissing and clawing and he put his finger to his mouth even as he let go of me. "Demons are on him too."

I knew that. I twisted in the air and flew hard toward Maks. I swept around the house between us, and saw him standing there, talking to . . . a ghost? The ghost took a step, and then stepped *into* Maks.

"Maks!" I yelled his name, forget being quiet. "Maks, no! No letting things in! Bad, bad idea!"

Robert was right behind me, knocking a demon out of the air as it launched at me. "I told you to be quiet!"

Of course, my yelling had done what we'd been trying to avoid all along. It brought the demons down on all of us.

Oops.

I flew straight toward Maks and slammed into his chest. "Don't let him in, it's a lie!"

Maks startled and his arms went around me even as he stumbled backward and the image of the ghost man popped out of him. The ghost man threw his hands in the air, his mouth moving with what looked like a string of curses. "Lila? Where's Zam? Is she okay?" Maks stared down at me. I'd stopped him from being possessed, at least.

I twisted about and saw the ghost of the other man fade away from sight. No, that wasn't quite right. "She's fine, last I saw her."

The air and light around us suddenly shifted. There was no sound to accompany the change. Above us the clouds turned silvery white, throwing light everywhere and dispersing the shadows as far as I could see. The demons that were crowding toward us screeched, the noise burrowing into my sensitive ears and I screamed right back, howling in pain.

Maks clamped an arm around me, and I let him hold me so I could focus on blocking out the noise.

Robert reached us and motioned for us to follow him. He might have spoken, but I couldn't be sure with all the fucking symphony going on.

Maks hesitated, and then we were running full tilt, headed north, until Robert ducked into what looked like had once been a church. The steeple was mangled, but still standing. Barely.

"Here." Robert crouched down. Even in the house

the light was brilliant, but the sound of the demons shrieking in pain was gone. "The light, that's my mother's doing. She is trying to help your friend, I'd bet."

I looked at Robert. "Soleil. But she was with Nico?"

Maks looked from me to Robert. "Who is he?"

I took a breath. "Short version is he is on our side, trying to stop Asag. Yes, I trust him. He knows Will."

Maks looked down at me. "Lila, that's not a reason to trust someone."

"Made me trust you when we first met, and I've yet to find my litmus test false," I said. "We need his help. He knows the truth about Asag. And all his friends. Robert, you tell him." I slid out of Maks's arms and flew across the room, over the pews and to the main pulpit. There were dead flowers and candles that had burned right down to their base, a bit of wax here and there.

A torn red cloth moved in a slight breeze. It hung over the pulpit, fluttering. In and out, in and out as though it were breathing.

I could hear Maks asking the same kind of questions I had, could hear his heartbeat change. "You didn't take Roshawn on?" Robert asked him.

"You know . . . Roshawn?" Maks answered the question with one of his own.

I hopped up on the pulpit to observe the two men.

Robert gave a nod. "He worked with me, to try and stop Asag. He was killed, I was . . . my mind was stilled. That is the only word I have for it. I believe that my mother likely stepped in to keep me from being destroyed. Someone had to give me a new name in order for me to be free of the curse."

The faint ghostly figure of the man I'd seen trying to go into Maks re-appeared. I couldn't hear him speaking, but I could see his mouth moving. No curses this time.

Maks nodded. "He's saying that we can trust you. Even if you are half-demon."

Robert shrugged. "If it was my choice, I'd renounce that part of me. As it is, I do what I can to offset my blood."

"And what are you suggesting?" Maks asked quietly. "You have a plan to get rid of Asag?"

"We need the same three things that he needs. In order for him to free himself fully from the curse I laid on him, trapping him in the castle, he needs the shifter girl—a specific one. The horn. And you, Jinn master. In order for us to stop him, we need the same three things. Irony, right? My mother would call it balance."

Maks leaned back against a pew as if we had all the time in the world. I could see the ghost next to him talking rapidly, hands flinging into the air.

"Oh, I agree fully. How do we know? I mean, if the same three things are needed both for him to succeed, and for us to succeed, why didn't someone just tell us that before we stepped foot into Trevalon? Or better yet, before we left the Storm Keep? Or why didn't anyone along the way fill us the fuck in?" Maks was close to shouting. And from him that was saying something—not really one to take to anger. It was unnerving to see him so pissed.

He was usually the calm one in our group.

Robert shrugged. "Because you were dealing with demons, and the minions of demons. Their job was to get you here, you schmuck, and like so many, *you've* fallen for it. You think those traps were just set up for you? Let me guess, Pazuzu and Mamitu told you that you were the first to get through? That no one had ever found their way through before?"

My heart picked up speed. "They did. But we found Vahab! He said we were the first too!"

Robert slowly shook his head. "I've been watching from the shadows and while I couldn't interact, I remember everything I've seen. How many Jinn men are missing? They weren't *all* killed. They were just stuffed into vases and crates and told it was because they were the strongest. Though I do remember Vahab. He was around then, and he was fighting hard against Asag. It wouldn't take much for you, or him, to believe that he was actually one of the strongest. Ego is a powerful thing, you know."

The ghost next to Maks had his jaw hanging, flapping in the wind if he'd been solid enough to have that actually happen.

"Are you . . . fucking kidding me?" Maks slumped, using the pew to hold himself up. Barely. "All this time . . . but why?"

I thought I might know the answer, though I didn't have to like it. "With dragons, we can't have the weak without the strong. There is an . . . order to life. Maybe it's the same with demons? Mamitu said it was about rules. That we had to follow the rules in order to make it all the way to Asag."

Robert nodded. "Close, and she wasn't lying about that bit. It is about rules: that much is true. And it's about balance. The rules are remarkably simple. In order to escape a curse, you must have the right tools. I gave my life to lock him away, as did Roshawn. The tools cannot be easy to gather, or what is the point of the curse in the first place?"

That bit Roshawn nodded along with. I realized that the ghost was becoming clearer. Which meant the light outside was getting darker.

"Hurry, we're losing the light." I hopped on top of the pulpit with the red tattered cloth. Silk, it was soft under the pads of my feet.

"When the time comes, Jinn," Robert looked at Maks, "you must take the unicorn horn. It will give you the strength to stop Asag. I can guide you on the spell you need to send him back to the realm of demons. Any demons attached to him will be taken along for the ride."

"And the girl, what about Reyhan?" I flew to land on Maks's shoulder. "You said she is a part of this too."

Robert gave a slow nod. "If she is the right girl,

then it is her blood that you'll need to cast the demons out."

"HER BLOOD?" I shrieked. "We can't . . . that's not okay! We aren't going to kill her!"

"It is the curse!" Robert snapped. "I am not the one who set that bounty. It came into existence on a piece of paper that literally appeared out of thin air! The cost of the curse, of removing it is heavy. Just as the cost of freeing Asag is as heavy!" He ran his hands over his hair. "There is only one sheet actually speaking about the cost of the curse, and it was in the hands of the Storm Queen, from what I heard."

I didn't think Maks could slump more. "We killed her," he said.

Robert's eyes bugged out and he slumped in the other direction. "You. . . killed Tamisa? We need her."

Maks and I shared a look. "No, we killed Dani."

Robert pushed off the pew, a tremble in his hands. "Thank the gods that are left to thank. Then there is only one thing ahead of us. We need to get you to the castle. But safely, and keep you hidden until we can get all three pieces together. We must do all we can to take Asag by surprise. Perhaps . . ."

"Reyhan is there," I said. "She and Fen were taken by Steven."

Robert grimaced. "In one way, that makes our job easier. If she is there, we must wait on your woman to bring the horn. She has it?"

I nodded. "In her bag."

"What about Steven? He was big, and I don't think we could face him unless Lila was able to shift back to her big size," Maks said.

Robert rolled his eyes. "Steven was always a bit of a prat. Never much liked him. He followed the rules to the point of hurting himself and those who depended on him. But he shouldn't be a problem. He is not a protector of Asag."

"Aren't we kind of doing the same thing?" I said.

"Different," Robert grumbled. "This is different. We are trying to keep everyone safe."

I wasn't sure that us following the rules was different, but what choice did we have right then? There was no other plan, no other way that I could see moving forward.

I spread my wings to fly toward Maks. As I lifted off, the light disappeared, and a slick shadow shot out from under the pulpit.

All I caught was the flutter of the red cloth. I rolled in the air as the demon's claws shot toward me, slicing across my belly.

Pain lit me up, red hot, and I worked to clamp it down, to hide it. Because I knew that if Zam felt my pain, she would come running. I gasped and lost altitude as the shadow fully pulled itself out from under the pulpit. "Ssssssuch wonderful planssssss," it whispered. "Assssssag will reward me for thisssssss."

I would have hit the ground if not for Maks. He lunged for me, catching me as I fell. My eyes rolled, and the last thing I saw was Roshawn, the ghost, pushing his way into Maks and Robert diving toward the demon.

This was not how I thought my day would end. Not by a long shot.

EIGHTEEN

ZAM

S oleil had not been lying. My run back through the demon city of Trevalon, headed south, was completely undisturbed.

She'd said to take the main road, straight toward the entrance that had been guarded by golems. Running for all I was worth, I let myself truly reach for Bryce.

I reached for my brother, my reserves and heart low. I didn't want him here, I didn't want him in this mess. But I needed him to bring me Balder.

And maybe, just maybe he could unblock the ability to shift.

Part one of my plan.

A boom erupted ahead of me. The massive gates were in the distance and I watched as they shuddered and exploded inward. I slid to a stop as my connection to my brother and our family opened wide.

They were here, inside the demon city.

I still couldn't shift to two legs.

Lilith still screeched inside my head like the goddess-damned banshee that she was.

Balder was in the lead of the rush of hooves, riderless, his coat glistening in the dim light. Dim light? I looked up to see that the skies were no longer the brilliant glowing clouds that had kept the demons at bay. Was that because of what Soleil had done?

Balder whinnied, turned on the speed, and ran straight for me. He covered the distance in no time, distance that would have taken me far too long.

As he drew close I leapt straight up and landed in the saddle. Bryce joined us a moment later, riding on the back of a true unicorn. Unicorn horns everywhere glistened.

And we had moments before the darkness closed in.

Fuck.

"Zamira."

"I'm stuck," I whispered, bowing my head. It had been a long time since I'd needed help to shift. "I've been pushed back and forth too many times."

My brother reached out, not with his hand, but with the power of an alpha. "Zamira, we all get stuck."

He didn't say it was okay, but his power flowed over me and settled into my bones, tugging my body back to two legs. Sure, the shift left me heaving off the side of Balder's back, struggling to breathe. A hand touched my back.

Kiara. "We are here. And we are ready to fight. The golems fell easily."

Which was the first thing that had me wincing. Soleil had not been lying. All along, there had been enough resistance to drive us, enough fear to keep us fighting. And it had been perfectly acted because we were not the first. We were just the first that brought Asag what he needed.

Fuck.

Suddenly, I wondered if that was why the Storm Queen had wanted her own unicorns? To take their horn . . . and stop Asag? Double fuck, if we'd been able to work with her, how much closer would we be?

"It's a trap," I said. "Bryce, this whole thing has been a trap to get . . . all the pieces here that Asag needs. Pazuzu is not on our side. It's why he wanted you and the unicorns to stay."

I patted Balder's neck. "Just me and my boy, and Dancer will go in from here. Asag . . . wants me to reach him. I'll be okay."

"He's tried to kill you!" Bryce snapped, his face filling with anger and concern.

"It's a game to him," I said. "One that I didn't have the rules to, but I think I do now. Or at least, I'm so fucking close I can taste the win on my lips." I grinned, forcing the smile to my face. "Bryce. You brought me hope, and you brought me the strength I needed, and a much-needed shift. Now I need you to leave. I need you to get the unicorns as far away as possible. They are the key to Asag escaping."

Even as we spoke, the light dimmed more. My anxiety spiked. "You have to go, now!"

My brother's amber eyes narrowed, and he stared hard at me. "And if you die?"

I shrugged. "Then I guess I'll just have to come and haunt your ass."

Kiara was shaking her head, but I knew she was not the one I had to convince. They led the pride together, but ultimately, this was his decision . . . "If this was a true war, would we be able to stand here and talk, Bryce? No, Asag would be on us. But it isn't a true war. He wants what I have. He needs it to free himself. And we need it to end him."

The ground below us shuddered.

There were a lot of things I could have done to send my brother and Kiara away. But it finally came down to the one thing that I knew he would listen to—the one thing that he cared for as much, or more, than me. The thing that I'd been shocked he would put in harm's way in the first place.

"As the alpha, you cannot risk the entire pride. You need to get all the unicorns out of here. As far from the demon city as you can. That won't just keep their horns out of his hands. But the pride too."

Bryce was not a stupid man—stubborn, absolutely, but not stupid.

"We came across the desert to find you, Zamira," he growled. "To find you and help you!"

"I know. And . . ." I scrunched up my eyes. Damn it, must be grit in the air to make them so watery. "And it did help me. You came, because you felt me in trouble, you came when I needed you most. You've helped me now. You brought me our horses. This, all of this was enough to give me the heart to keep going. Please, believe me when I say that you have to go. You have to. This was a trap, one that I walked into, and I can't take the rest of you all the way into it."

Bryce and Kiara shared a look, the look that only mates can interpret.

"We will wait, out by the ocean, where we arrived," he said. "If you aren't out in one day, we are coming in after you."

My heart clenched. "Don't."

"You don't think you'll make it?" Kiara stared hard at me, and I made myself smile.

"No idea. But my life is not worth all of theirs. We all know this."

Bryce pushed the unicorn he rode close to me and Balder. "Not true, sister. Not true at all. We will ride back with those willing to come if you aren't back in a day. One day."

I knew him, and I knew that I'd pushed as far as I could without physically restraining him. "Deal."

A nod from him, and a tearful smile from Kiara, and that was it. "Let's move." He gave the orders and though the pride was there, ready to fight, they turned. I watched as the rode away.

Leaving me, Balder and Dancer on our own. Well, not quite on our own.

My crazy uncle Shem stood there, as the unicorns kicked up the hard-packed earth. "Thought you might need a little more help."

"You should go," I sighed, already knowing he was coming with me.

"Should, could, won't." He leapt up onto Dancer's back. "The thing is, I feel . . . compelled to come this way. Have for a lot of years. Something is calling to me." He squinted ahead of us, through the semi-darkness to the castle. "So that's how it is."

As a shaman of our pride, he did have a little magic. Not much, but maybe it would be the edge we needed.

I patted Balder's neck. "You and me, buddy. We're going to ride into this together."

He snorted and popped up on his back feet, striking at the air. I knew him, I knew he'd be up for the fight. "You too, Dancer." I reached over and touched the black mare's hip and she bobbed her head too.

"And me." Shem waved at me as if I'd forgotten him.

I took his waving hand and squeezed it. "I am glad for your company."

I watched the pride, Bryce and Kiara ride away, my heart pounding.

"Hurry," I yelled. "Get the hell out of here!"

Balder let out a sharp whinny and the unicorns took off, full speed, nearly dumping most of their riders.

I patted his neck. "Good boy."

He snorted and pawed the ground, and I could almost feel his thoughts against mine again. Not possible without my magic coming back to me, but I'd take it.

"Ready to run? We have ground to cover, as fast as we can."

Shem saluted me. "I am ready."

I hadn't been asking him, but his presence gave me a strange bit of comfort.

There was not a moment to lose now. We had to get to Maks and Lila, and then we headed straight to Asag.

Even if you have the pieces to the spell, you do not have the spell itself. Fool. Idiot. Dumb ass.

Time to play the game. "I've had it all along, Lilith. You're not the only one who can lie through her teeth. You aren't the only one who can manipulate the fuck out of someone."

Her shocked silence resounded.

Shem shot me a look and I shook my head. I didn't have time to explain . . . "I have a new weapon, not unlike the flail." There, maybe I did have a little time.

I kept my other more traitorous thoughts to myself. Like the fact that I had no such thing. I had no spell. But she didn't know that.

Where would the spell be? That was the one thing that Soleil hadn't been able to tell me.

Balder was running full tilt, and I scanned the ground for traps. But the main road was bare of anything. Clear and flat, ready to run down.

Ready for Asag to have what he wanted brought to him.

All the discussions that we'd face an army, false.

Every fucking prophecy, false.

Every demon we'd dealt with, liars.

So now we had to play this game harder, and more ruthless than ever before.

And hope to all that was holy that we didn't screw it up.

I leaned into Balder as Dancer raced alongside us. "We got this, right?"

He flicked one ear back to me, and then forward again. Yeah, he wasn't sure either.

But I couldn't let Lilith know that. So instead, I taunted the shit out of her.

"Asag actually thinks he's hidden our magic well, doesn't he?" I laughed and shook my head. "I think your lover brother is the fool, not me."

Her anger simmered as we galloped along and after a few minutes she broke.

You cannot break his vault. No one ever has!

"First time for everything," I laughed. "I'm a master thief, Lilith. I stole the gems of power for years, bringing them back to Ishtar. I was her go-to girl." I let the laughter spill into my words. "Asag won't even know what hit him."

To say she did not like that was an understatement. Her wrath bubbled and writhed inside of me but I pushed her away and thought only of my plan.

A vault then? A vault could be broken into. Our magic restored. Save Reyhan and Fen. Then to find the spell, and deal with Asag. After that, all the dragons would be free.

I swallowed hard at the tasks ahead of me. One of them on their own would be enough to make me hesitate.

"We got this," I whispered into the wind, lying to myself now. "We got this."

NINETEEN

REYHAN

I woke up, feeling warm, with a full belly and . . . "Oh, my head hurts," I whispered as I rolled over and the world spun in a way that not only hurt my head, but my belly too. On my hands and knees, I stayed where I was as the feeling passed. "Fen?"

"Here. I also am not feeling well either," he grumbled. "But now that we are back on this side of sleep, we need to find what it was that our friend wanted us to find. She said that it was in here, somewhere . . ."

"The key to stopping Asag was in here, that's what she said." I sat up and was glad that the world was moving normally now. "What kind of key, do you think?"

Fen wobbled across the carpeted floors. "I doubt it's an actual key. Maybe a weapon that could kill him? Or a poison perhaps?"

I pursed my lips and slowly stood. "Why didn't he find us?"

Fen looked around, his wings fluttering and his tail shaking a little. "This room is protected, I can feel the Jinn magic all over it. So that must be something of a weakness to him," he said. "But even so, let's keep our voices low."

That was a good idea. Not that I felt like shouting, not in the least. Nope. No shouting here. I walked around the room, letting my fingers trail over the different items. Over the cushions and the dusty table tops, over the bits and pieces of jewelry. I found a tiny knife, one that fit my hand. I liked how it felt against my palm.

"What about this?"

Fen flew up to land carefully on the top of my head. His claws scratched in a most lovely way that made me want to close my eyes and lean into the itchiness. My mom used to scritch my head like that. "It's a good knife. Put it in the top of your boot, so you have a weapon. Though I don't think it's magical, do you?"

He was right, there was no magic tingle or anything to the knife.

He pushed off and flew around the big room, and we both kept looking. The necklaces, I couldn't resist trying them on and looking in the full-length mirror. "Was that lady Tamisa . . . was she the demon's mate?"

"No, I doubt that." Fen landed on the top of a big

dresser with doors big enough that I could crawl inside and . . .

A boom on the door *behind* me sent us running straight for the cupboard. I had the door open and I slid inside, crouching down between one breath and the next. Fen slipped in through the crack as the main door boomed again, the whole structure shuddering.

"I hear you in there, little one. I will have your blood. One way or another!" the demon roared, his voice coming through loud and terrible.

The wood of the door creaked and groaned.

But whatever magic was holding it together did not give way to the demon's blows. I pulled back further, ducking under the long shirts and dresses within the standing closet. "Will it hold?" I whispered as low and quiet as I could to Fen.

He stayed where he was at the crack, staring out across the room. Did he see wood chips flying? Did he see pieces of the door being blown apart? I closed my eyes, tears leaking out.

"So far," Fen whispered back.

But the booms, the attack on the door continued.

"The door shudders, but it's not breaking." Fen crawled up into my lap. "Kid. If we can get to a window, I can fly us out of here. Okay? That's what we need to do. We need to escape."

I sniffed and rubbed at my nose. "Okay, but what about Zam and Lila and Maks . . ." Even if I didn't know

Maks well, I did know he was Zam's mate. Which made him important too.

"They are grown-ups, they don't need our help." Fen patted my cheek gently. "If we get out of here, then they have less to worry about."

I frowned. "But Tamisa said the key to stopping the bad guy is in here somewhere." I shifted my weight. Something hard and pointed was digging into my hip. My fingers drifted down to what turned out to be a small box. I scooted over.

My eyesight wasn't as good as when I was in my cat form, but still better than the average kid. I picked up the box in one hand, silk scarves sliding off to reveal deep blue paint, stars and a crescent moon etched into the top. "Fen. We have to help them. We just have to."

I was speaking to him as I stared at the box. The crescent moon held my eyes in a way that I didn't understand. I fumbled with the latch that held the lid closed. Fen spun around. "What is this?"

"I don't know. But I . . ." I popped the latch and a sigh slid out of the box. A woman's sigh. Mist poured out of the box, filling the closet space, like fog. Like the fog that had been over the city. The scent of flowers and sea salt came with it, and for just a moment it felt like I was standing on the edge of the ocean, staring out at the waves.

I couldn't move as a woman appeared in the mist, slowly taking form. I stared up at her. "Storm Queen."

"I was, once." Her body and face looked like the one

who had hurt us but no, this was different. "My body is trapped here, in the castle. This is just a memory."

"Tamisa?" Fen asked her.

She bowed her head. "I am the oldest daughter of Queen Mariallas, Storm Queen for over five hundred years. She sent me with the spell to deal with Asag." Her form wavered. "I failed."

"Why?" Fen asked. "What can we do different?"

"There are items you need to banish him. A Jinn master. The horn of a unicorn, and the blood of a shifter's child. And one other." She bent down and whispered it to me, right in my ear. "That is the key, little one. The key that Asag himself does not know of. It is the hope I can give you to stop him."

The word rattled around in my head. I opened my mouth, and her ghostly hand covered my lips. "You must not speak it out loud. Even I, sharing it with you, is deadly dangerous. For if he hears, then all hope of stopping him will be gone like fog under the sun."

I swallowed the word. "What should I do?"

"The four items must be taken together, and the words of binding spoken." She motioned toward the box. "Do you see it?"

I reached into the night sky box and pulled out a fragile piece of paper. I read the words over a few times. "Should I memorize them?"

"Yes." Her voice was fading. "Remember them, both of you. In the belly of the castle is a scrying mirror. Over that must the binding be created . . . or broken. Only then will you be able to cast him out forever."

The words were not long. I read them over and over. "Fen, help me. I don't want to forget." Even as I spoke the paper was disintegrating in my hands. Falling to pieces. This was what we needed to stop the demon.

The main door boomed, as if Asag knew that we were gaining something on him. "Little cat, I will kill you yet!"

I bit my lower lip and read the lines over and over again, until there was nothing left to read. Ashes stuck to my fingers as if the paper had burned away in my hands. Even though there was nothing left of it, I carefully wiped my hands over the box, so the ashes went back in.

The spirit memory of the Storm Queen was gone now.

Fen tapped my knee with the tip of his tail. "There are four things? The first three . . . the others are bringing them. The horn. The master, that will be Maks." He didn't say anything about the shifter child. He didn't have to. I knew it was me. I was young in some ways, and in others . . . not so much.

I nodded. "I need . . . to search the castle. Fen. We have to find it. The scrying mirror."

The booming on the door was not letting up this time. "It's only a matter of time, I would think, till he gets through. We need to find another way out. Do you have any idea where this other item might be?"

I swallowed hard. "We need to get to the demon's personal spaces. I . . . I think it will be there."

Fen let out a groan. "Are you sure?"

I nodded. "Yes. Sorry."

"Don't apologize, this is not your fault, or even mine," he sighed. "Can you shift if you need to?"

I closed my eyes and felt my way to where my body would slide to four feet if I needed. "Yes, the sleep helped."

Fen made his way out of the closet first. I kept the small box tucked under my arm, but of course I couldn't take it with us. "Thank you," I whispered as I put it back, hiding it under the pile of silks.

"Be careful," her voice floated around us. "I will help if I can."

Sliding out of the closet, I crouched to the floor as the door in front of me bowed inward. Deep red sparkling magic curled around it, bending and pushing on the door.

Fen made a motion with his tail, circling around and around. Search the room? Yes, maybe there was another way out. There had to be.

Each boom of the door had me cringing, but Fen and I did not slow. We went on opposite sides of the room, touching the walls, moving the silken hangings, looking for anything that would give us a way out. A secret door. A tiny hole even. There were no windows. No other doors. No secret doors even.

Tears threatened. I was too little; I wasn't good at this. Hiding I could do, even running and escaping. But I was too little for this job!

A sob escaped me as I slid to my knees. The thick rugs cushioned me at least as I lay down and curled into a ball. The rattling of the door was so steady now it didn't even make me jump.

"Reyhan, listen to me," Fen whispered. "We must keep trying. That last thing she told you, without it . . . we can't beat him without it. We must do this."

I curled my fingers into the rugs, hating that he was right. I knew we had to keep trying. Where else could there be a place to escape this room?

I sat up as the thought hit me. I didn't speak, just pointed at the rugs. At the floor. A trapdoor maybe? It was a small hope.

Fen's eyes lit up and he jumped up and down in excitement. Together we started pulling back the layers of rugs. Was this why there were so many? To act as a deterrent. Because who would make it so difficult to get to an escape door? Hope flared in my chest, and I followed my instincts. More than that, I followed my nose. There was a puff of fresh air sliding up and around us as we pulled back more and more rugs.

The bare stone floor finally looked back at us. More than that was the tiny indentation that indicated that maybe this was more than just a floor. I took a breath, dug my fingers into the indent and pulled.

It moved! The trapdoor moved silently, opening just wide enough of a space for a single body.

The main door cracked and groaned, and as we looked to it, we could see through to the other side.

The demon's laughter was clear as day. "Tamisa, you little bitch, I knew I'd break your door one day!"

"Go, go!" Fen pushed me into the darkness. "I'll cover this back up; wait for me at the top of the ladder."

I'd not even noticed the ladder; the banging on the door, the threat of the demon was too much. I did as Fen said, taking hold of the top rung and swinging myself down and into the inky darkness of the escape tunnel. I pulled the lip of the trapdoor down, holding it just a crack open so Fen could join me. And then the weight of the rugs being piled back on pushed on me.

I gritted my teeth and held my position, my thin arms shaking as more and more weight was added. How many rugs were there? It didn't matter, not really. I wasn't going to leave Fen behind.

I couldn't do this without him.

Through the layers of rugs, I could hear the demon screaming. What if he walked on the trapdoor? I wouldn't be able to hold it up and he'd feel me give way.

Hurry, Fen, hurry, was all I could think, mouthing

the words but not willing to say them out loud and somehow draw the demon's attention to me.

As the last of my strength slid from me, hands slick with sweat, two sets of tiny claws shot through the narrow space and then Fen was dragging himself into the darkness with me. I lowered the trapdoor the last few inches, grateful that Fen was a skinny dragon. Grateful that he'd made it.

As the trapdoor sealed shut, all the sound from above stopped. The screaming and the booms were as if they had never been, and with the quiet my fears calmed a little. Fen slid down my back and then began to make his way down the ladder. I followed, moving carefully, like the ghost had said. Slowly because my arms were aching, and my hands were still sweaty.

The trick now would be wherever this let out, we'd have to find our way to the demon's bed chamber. A place I really didn't want to go. But my family needed us to be strong, and brave. And even if I was terrified, I would fight for them.

That was all there was to it.

CHAPTER
TWENTY

ZAM

As we rode, I looked across at my uncle.

"I don't think we're getting out of this." I blurted the words out. "In case you want to turn back now. I would understand."

There it was, the first time I'd said what I'd been feeling all along, out loud. That this was the last adventure for me, that it was the last time I'd ride my Balder, that it was the last time I'd face darkness.

What are you going to do? I can feel you thinking, but I cannot see your thoughts. Lilith's words rumbled through me. *You cannot possibly know where the spell is hidden.*

"But you aren't giving up yet?" Shem tipped his head sideways. I smiled, though it was rough around the edges, and I wasn't sure that it would convince him that what I was going to say wasn't terrible.

"I have an idea," I said. It was a crazy fucking

idea. One that was a thousand times crazier than negotiating with Asag the first time, for more time. But that was before I knew what I was up against. Before I knew that this was truly a game, one that had deadly results, but a game nonetheless. "Trust me."

"I do, of course I trust you," Shem said. "But that doesn't tell me what the plan is."

But I wasn't sure that it was for Shem that I spoke, or for Lilith. I would need her to trust me—in a distinct moment where she shouldn't.

And I had to make her believe that my lies were truth and my truth lies. What a fucking mess.

"Let's go. This straight path, Balder, might have sand traps in it." I urged him with my heels to the closest side street where I could show him one of the sand traps. There weren't many. Which again told me that at least some of what Soleil had passed on to me was correct. The traps were ahead of me.

The demons were ahead of me.

Asag had yet to figure out where we were.

Balder and Dancer both dropped their noses to the one we found, and gave it a sniff. Nothing responded from inside—all the demons were gone. Headed north, thinking I was out that way.

"That's what they look like. Can you spot them on the fly?" I leaned over so I could get a good look in his eye. He pawed at the trap and then from a standstill, leapt over it.

Dancer followed and Shem grunted as they landed. "Could have had some warning," he wheezed out.

I guess that was the answer. "There is less than a day's ride for us if we go hard to get to the castle," I said. "You two ready?"

The two hornless unicorns took off full tilt, I didn't even have to urge them. Shem barely hung on, but he managed.

Riding like this, leaning into the wind, letting Balder run at his top speed was everything I needed after the last few days of misery in the darkness, of avoiding demons and fighting against an impossible deadline. For the moment, I was strangely at peace, despite what lay ahead of us.

I let my senses reach out for my family. Bryce and Kiara were riding hard, away from us, back toward the ocean and then veering to the west.

Maks was . . . he was with Lila still.

I could feel them together, ahead of me. Close to the castle, though how close I wasn't sure.

Changing who I was sensing, I reached for Fen and Reyhan. They were still straight north. Still within the castle as far as I could tell. Not afraid, a bit uncertain but alive and well.

I had no doubt that Asag had somehow lost them.

I reached a little further, letting myself sink into my connection with them, kind of like casting a net to see if one of them could reach back for me.

Because I had to pass on what I'd learned. Just in

case I . . . didn't make it. Goddess of the desert, I did not want to think like that.

Reyhan was the first to respond, surprising me. Her thoughts were scattered, dancing across my own, and like a child's drawing I had to interpret what she was telling me.

She had the spell in the box and there were four things, not three that we needed. The fourth was . . . a jewel?

Fuck me, please let it not be one of the gems of power.

I sent her a soft, gentle touch as best I could. Told her to keep looking, but stay safe.

She fed me the lines of the spell, frantic, fear driving her.

INTO THE VOID, *into the mirror*
    Speak freely this, then speak it clearer
    Demons lost, demons found
    This demon here, must now be bound
    Cast to depths, into the realm
    This demon goes, and n'er is found.

"GOOD JOB, REYHAN!" I whispered out loud. "Stay safe, you don't have to keep looking."

Her instant response was she was no lady, and would damn well do as she pleased and that meant helping.

Gods, I loved that kid. "Be careful!"

Lila was the next one to respond.

Her mind touched mine, and her words flowed over me. That they were working with a half demon, and that he'd told them exactly what Soleil had told me.

The patterns were becoming clear, at least.

"I'm on my way," I said out loud, and felt her turn toward us. Maks too, but he felt . . . different? I couldn't quite put my finger on the sensation, but he was off. Maks but not.

Lila's thoughts were jumbled after that, more like feelings and impressions. As though she were . . . injured? Something poisoned her? Was that it?

Fuck. "Balder, we need to get Maks and Lila," I yelled into the wind. The end of this game was fast approaching and we could not lose each other before we faced Asag.

No more separating, no more running around like chickens whose heads had been lopped off.

Time to pull our shit together, and tackle Asag as a team. "Shem. Don't fall off, I can't stop for you!"

"I would expect nothing less, niece!" he hollered back.

Good enough.

Balder's stride suddenly changed, and I felt his muscles bunch to take another leap. He stumbled on something—maybe a rock, maybe the start of the booby trap. He went down to one knee; I was thrown up on his neck and clung to him as he still managed to leap.

It was a trap! Fucking demons! I held my breath as we sailed through the air, and it left me in a whoosh as we landed on the other side. I let go of his neck and hit the dirt, knocking the wind out of me and rolling out of Balder's way.

He scrambled hard, his back end hanging inside the trap.

"Shem, help me!" I grabbed at Balder's bridle and jaw and a piece of his mane, leaning back, giving him all I could to help him get his ass out of the hole.

Shem managed to grab the front edge of the saddle, and between the three of us we got Balder out of the hole. I fell backward as my boy stood there, shaking, his sides heaving.

He could run for hours upon hours, but fear was a different beast. One that took a whole other kind of toll on the body and mind.

"You okay?" I rubbed the side of his face, grateful his tack hadn't broken. I'd have lost him then. I swallowed the lump in my throat. "We still have to go, as quick as we can. Can you do it?"

He blew a hot blast of air into my face and gave me a bump. I checked his saddle and straps, checked that my saddlebags were still there, touched the bag I carried, feeling the horn inside of it. Then I mounted.

"Watch for a shimmer in the sand!" I said as I

settled my balance once more in the saddle. That was the best we could do. Four sets of eyes looking for the booby traps.

We rode hard for two hours easily, not slowing, taking every trap laid out as if it was nothing. Even though I felt the tension rolling off Balder, seeing it in the foaming sweat that coated his sides.

Demons popped out here and there, but they couldn't come close to catching us. Fucking right they weren't able to—Balder and Dancer were too fast.

I let my mind work over that two-hour period—there was nothing to do but think, and as I went through everything, it only made our situation worse.

My plan was simple. It would work, but we had to get to Asag. And Reyhan had to get to the mirror.

He would expect us to go for the vault, I wanted him to believe that. "I'm going to get my magic back," I let myself mutter over and over. Lilith was quiet but she was listening. Exactly as I wanted.

My guts twisted. We should never have trusted—even though we hadn't fully trusted—Nico and Soleil. My guts twisted further as I realized we were doing it again.

All of us were trusting Soleil that she was trying to stop Asag, that she and her son—this Robert fellow—were somehow against the other demons.

"How do you know?" I yelled in sheer frustration. How the fuck were we supposed to know who was with us, and who wasn't?

I would have sworn that Mamitu and Pazuzu were on our side. And yet now looking at how they'd pushed us, I wondered how I had missed the signs. They had acted their roles to nothing short of perfection.

We weren't the first to come this way, there was nothing special about us. We were up against a monster who'd caged dragons, and who had put an entire portion of the world under his thumb. All so he could find the three things he needed to free himself from the cage that Soleil's son had put him in.

Four, if Reyhan was right.

A jewel of some sort.

Dread began to pool in the place where my guts had previously twisted. We'd survived so much.

But we'd had some power to our names. Maks's Jinn abilities. My growing Jinn abilities. Lila's size and strength.

Balder leapt another trap and nearly unseated me. I struggled to get my foot back in a stirrup as unbalanced as I was because my mind was elsewhere.

No, I couldn't let my thoughts go there. I locked onto Lila's energy.

And felt her slipping away. The poison was working quickly.

"No," I breathed the word. No, why had Maks not said anything? Maybe he didn't realize how she was dying? But how could he not?

I reached for him, scrambling to connect to his mind. But he . . . he wasn't there? I could sense him, but it was like the space where he should have been was gone. What the fuck was going on?

"Balder, hurry faster." I gave a low hiss to him, and squeezed him with my legs. He found another gear, and we both leaned into it.

Dancer thundered along beside us, neck outstretched, Shem's eyes locked on the ground in front of us. He didn't ask why we'd suddenly picked up more speed. I wouldn't have heard the question over the rushing of the wind in my ears anyway.

Following the threads to my family, I felt Maks and Lila now to my right, and I sat deep and leaned back to change speed. Balder almost sat down trying to slow himself, grit and sand flying up around us, and then we were turning to the right, galloping between houses, weaving our way through and past rubble to get to them.

To get to Lila and Maks.

A man I didn't recognize popped out of the house directly in front of us. Blue eyes, dark hair, he had the look of Soleil about him, enough that I knew this would be the one that Maks had said was helping them.

"You must be Zam." He tipped his head. "My mother was helping—"

"Where's Lila?" I barked. "Get on the horse with him." I motioned to Dancer. If this one was coming with us, we needed to move.

Maks was next out of the building—what I realized

now wasn't a house but a church with the steeple not just broken, but turned upside down. Fucking demons.

He lifted his eyes to me and I knew that we were dealing with a goddess-be-buggered mess. "What the fuck? Who is in you, Maks?"

He tipped his head. "Roshawn."

"For fuck's sake, did you even notice that Lila was injured?" I actually should have cared more that we would end up calling down demons on us, but I didn't. Nope not one fucking bit.

The only thing that mattered was Lila and Maks. Because as soon as I had Lila straightened out, I would be grabbing hold of Maks and shaking him till Roshawn fucked right off.

CHAPTER TWENTY-ONE

I grabbed at Maks, and he held up Lila. "She's sleeping. I know that she was tired."

"She's not fucking sleeping!" I snapped as I curled my small friend, the sister of my heart, into my arms. Her breathing was labored and her scales, usually so warm, were cooling rapidly.

"Maks, I need you here." I pointed to Balder's back and he leapt up behind me. "We're going to have to do this on the fly."

Giving Balder his head, I asked him for speed once more. I barely noticed as he wove his way out from between the buildings to the main road. "The saddle-bags!" I yelled, reaching for the one on my back. "I'll use the horn."

If you use all the juice up, how are you going to banish him? Lilith whispered.

"I don't fucking know!" I snapped back at her. She

of course would want me to not use the horn. Her brother needed it. But we also needed it.

Maks, or should I say Roshawn, didn't hand me the horn. I twisted in the saddle as we galloped along. He had untied the saddlebag and . . . "Fucker!"

He leapt off Balder's back. Saddlebags in hand.

Balder slid to a stop, and I stared down at Maks as he shook his head. "I cannot allow you to take the one chance we have and throw it away, not even for her life."

"She is one of the keys!" I yelled at him. "So we are at an impasse."

Shem cleared his throat and I pointed a finger at him. "Not right now!"

"I think it rather important, niece," Shem said.

Maks snapped his fingers on his free hand, and a curl of green smoke wrapped around his body, enclosing him completely.

"Maks, you have to fight him!" I yelled as I clutched Lila a little tighter. "Lila will die if you don't! Roshawn, we need her too!"

"There are other dragons," his voice called out of the smoke. "The dragon's queen . . . queen is another word for a female dragon of breeding age."

"But none that are the daughter of the king," I yelled back.

Robert cleared his throat. "Give her to me. I can heal her. It is a demon's poison; if she'd said something earlier, I could have cleared it off her. There will be a cost, but not a big one."

That last part? Yeah, I didn't care if it cost me every last bit of my magic as long as Lila was okay.

The green smoke faded off from around Maks and I stared hard at him. Did he have the unicorn horn? No, he didn't. But he'd been willing to protect it against Lila needing it, which was absolutely shit.

"Don't you move a fucking inch!" I snapped at Maks. Roshawn, whatever. I pointed a finger at him for good measure.

You could cut his head off, Lilith whispered. I rolled my eyes, not bothering to even answer her.

Roshawn ignored me and opened the bag, his body stiffening. "Where is the horn? He said it was in here!"

"Let Maks go," I said. "Maks. I need you take back control."

Lila let out a little moan, but I didn't dare take my eyes off Maks. He was visibly struggling, his muscles flexing and dancing, his face in a tight grimace.

"Lila, you still with me?"

"Barely." She coughed, and it sounded wet.

"Watch the acid," I reminded her and hopefully warned Robert in time.

Shem cleared his throat. "If I may suggest, the fact that we are drawing a great deal of attention to us, that I don't think you want, so unless I'm wrong, perhaps we can discuss while running for our lives?"

Roshawn—for sure he was not Maks in that

moment—shook his head. "Damn you! I am the one who must wield the horn!"

"Yeah, and what are the words to the spell?" I countered as Robert stuffed a shivering Lila into my arms. I mounted up on Balder and Robert hopped up behind Shem, which left Roshawn to come with me.

Cursing a blue streak, he ran and leapt up onto Balder's back, his arms going around my waist.

"I know the words!"

"Really? 'Cause so do I, you dumb jerk! We are supposed to be working together." I gave a quick press of my heels to Balder's sides, and we were off and running, Dancer with Shem and Robert right behind us.

And just in time. The demons were all around us now and closing in fast. Watching them, though, I could see them holding back. Just barely, but they were holding back.

There were enough of them behind and to the sides of us, that we were being driven in a particular direction—right for the main gate of Asag's castle.

"She is correct," Robert called across to us. "We have to work together, Roshawn. Much as I know you like to play the hero, we need you to help us now."

Behind me Roshawn tensed and then a shudder ran through him. "Sorry."

Maks. He was back, I could hear it in his voice.

"What the hell?"

"I still have him in me, but I had to push him

down," Maks said, his arms tightening around me. "He does want to stop Asag, he's just not good at working with people."

The snort that exploded out of Robert said it all. This was not news to him.

The demons pressed in a little closer, which forced us to pick up more speed. "It's all a game," I said. "They are driving us toward him now."

Maks tensed. "Roshawn says that Asag will be bored. He is done with the entertainment, so will seek to end this quickly."

I blew out a breath and reached for my connection to Reyhan and Fen. Same as before, perhaps a little more confusion but otherwise they were doing good.

Lila moaned and forced herself up to my shoulder.

"I feel like shit."

I let myself connect to her through the bonds that tied us together—she wasn't dying now. She was tired, and her body ached, but she was alive.

Maks tucked closer. "I'm sorry, Lila, Roshawn had me under him, I couldn't—"

"Next time I tell you not to let a ghost in, maybe listen, okay?" she grumbled up at him, and took a swing at him with one wing.

He reached around and put his hand against her. "I am sorry, Lila."

She bit him, but it was not hard. Just enough to make her literal point.

"Look, we are going to be there in less time than it

feels right now. I have a plan," I said. Robert shot me a look and I made myself give him a wink. "Our magic is wrapped up in his vault, we are going for that first."

Yes, my voice carried, yes, I fully knew that the demons and thus Asag would hear me.

My plan depended on it.

"How are we going to get the castle doors to drop?" Robert asked. "There is a moat of lava if I recall correctly."

"Lava?" Shem spluttered. "Well and truly, lava?"

I nodded. "I'll force Lilith to turn into another kind of weapon, and I will throw her against the chains." Again, no idea if the chains were visible, but I needed Asag to think he would have my game plan. "Once the doors are down, we all head straight for the vault. Lilith is going to help us find it."

I will do no such thing! I am not going to help you get your magic back! Lilith shrieked and I smiled.

"You most certainly are."

The next three hours were nothing but running flat out. There were no more traps ahead of us, and no demons waiting to spring a trap. Robert was right—Asag was done with his game, bored, or just now wanting to be done with his curse. No matter the reason, his demons weren't stopping us.

As the castle loomed ahead of us, the turrets and brick visible for the first time in detail, I couldn't help but gasp at the scope of it.

Easily the building was the size of a small mountain, rising up in front of us in both height and depth. The thing was . . . bigger than the city we'd just run through, if what I was seeing was correct. I mean, in theory I'd understood that being able to see it at such a distance meant it was massive, but seeing it right up close and personal was a whole other can of worms.

I bent my head so that I spoke quietly to Lila. "The gate, can you drop it? Use your acid on the chains?"

She nodded and climbed slowly to my shoulder. "Yeah, I got some left."

Maks leaned his head against my back. "He's trying to take me over again."

"Tell him to get stuffed, we have work to do. Roshawn, you can come forward when the time is right, or better yet just hand your magic to Maks. I can give him the spell," I said over my shoulder.

"Shem." I looked across at my uncle. "When we find Reyhan, you protect her. She's only a little girl, and she's mine."

He bobbed his head, eyes serious. "You got it."

Maks startled. "Did you want to tell me something?"

"You think that I could leave her out in the world, without a parent?" I asked.

"No, never," he answered without hesitation, which was smart of him. "So she's ours?"

His words warmed me. "She's ours."

The wind blew toward us, bringing a sharp scent of

sulphur and the heat off the lava. "That's going to be a bitch to get past, even with a bridge," Shem said.

"When the drawbridge is down," I said, "we gallop across at full speed. Everyone hold your breath."

Goddess only knew what fumes would be rolling out of the lava.

The wind pushed toward us again and my skin tingled with the heat. "Fuck, it's time."

TWENTY-TWO

The ladder dropped us quite deep into the castle, so deep that to me it felt like we were going to get squashed. I hunched my shoulders.

"Funny," Fen said quietly. "There is light down here."

I looked around and saw the flickering bits of light here and there. "Magic lights?"

"Maybe, or just maybe a natural glow worm. I'm not sure." He didn't leave me to go investigate. "I wonder if this place was where Tamisa came in?"

Tamisa? It took me a moment to remember the name of the woman whose room we'd searched. "But why would she want to come here?"

"To stop Asag." Fen dropped to the floor and kept pace beside me. I missed his warmth, but I didn't miss how heavy he felt.

"Right." I nodded. "I remember."

Fen gave me a quick look. "You feeling okay, kid?"

I sniffed and nodded. "Let's find the things."

The mirror. The ring that belonged to Asag. How were we supposed to find them both? I could just sense Zamira not far from us now, and closing in. She gave me some of her strength and I drew in a breath. "I think that we should split up. You should find the mirror, and I'll go find the other thing."

He snorted. "That's a terrible idea, and it sounds like something an adult with a complex of needing to prove themselves would say. Not a smart kid like you. No, we stick together. We move fast. That's all there is to it." Fen hopped up and flew a loop around me. "The mirror is somewhere down here, right?"

I nodded. "I think so."

"Then we find it first." He flew ahead of me, teasing me along, and pretty quickly I was running to keep up with him. The walls and the floor were solid stone, and there were no offshoots to other room, or other directions that I could see. In fact . . .

"Does it feel like we are going deeper?"

"It does," Fen said. As he spoke a puff of his breath was visible. It was getting cold too, then.

"We just go faster," I said, and hurried along as best I could on two feet. Four feet would have been faster for sure, but I was not used to shifting so much. I wasn't sure it was a good idea to do it again unless I had to.

My dad had always told me to be careful about how often I shifted, and to only do it as needed. Or I'd get stuck and need an alpha to pull me out of it.

There was no alpha here, so I wasn't going to press my luck.

"Slow down." Fen flew back to me, slamming into my chest. "Someone is ahead."

I squeaked and the very rule I'd been thinking to stick to evaporated from my head. There was nowhere to hide. Nowhere to go. Would the person ahead be bothered by a small cat? Probably not.

But a little girl? That would not go unnoticed. I looked to Fen. "Should I shift?"

He shook his head. "Wait here, I'll check it out."

Dropping to the ground, he scuttled forward, hugging the wall. I pinned my back to the wall and wished some of the glow worms weren't so glowy.

Now that I was still, I could just hear the humming of someone up ahead. Humming? Singing almost.

Who would be singing in a place like this?

I reached up the wall to the glow worm closest to me and forced myself to grab it and throw it back the way we'd come. A few more, and I'd created a nice little shadow spot for me that might *maybe* save me if I had to shift.

I held very still. The singing had stopped.

Fen reappeared and I realized that he had gone around a corner.

He leapt up into my arms and put his mouth close

to my ear. "The mirror is in the room, but there is a rather angry looking beast guarding it."

"Is it small?" I whispered back.

"No, it's big, blocky and stupid looking," Fen said.

"The mirror?"

"Oh, shit, no—that's small enough you could carry it. I meant the thing guarding it."

I crept forward to get a look at the thing.

The turn was almost invisible with all the rock walls blending together. My fingers found it first and I peeked around to see just another hall.

Fen urged me on and I made my feet move, creeping silently. At the next juncture there were three directions. Fen pointed to the left and I moved around that corner. Ahead of us was a door, not quite closed.

Average sized, it didn't make me think there would be anything big behind it.

Fen didn't say a word, just motioned for me to look.

The urge to shift was strong, but I knew I would need my fingers to get hold of the mirror.

Near to the door, I slowed even further until I was barely moving. But this was how to stalk prey, and no matter how big the creature was inside, it was just another kind of prey.

I swallowed hard, at the edge of the door, and looked in. The creature was sitting sideways to the door.

Big and bulky indeed, it looked like it was made of clay, or bread dough; its skin was nearly translucent and you could see blue and red veins running all over its body.

More than that, sitting it was at least two men high.

A giant? A stubby kind of giant maybe? The top of his head was covered in a thick patch of white hair that sparkled on the ends. It was kind of pretty.

The face swung our way and I stepped back and held my breath.

"Whosa there?" The voice of the strange giant was thick and full of mucous. In fact, it spit and the edge of the door was covered in slime.

Fen and I didn't move.

"Baddling rats is gonna gonna die!"

And then it screamed. A bellow that shrieked from one octave to another and forced me to put my hands over my ears.

Horrendous.

Who had put this beast here? Tamisa? Asag? It was guarding the mirror, so I had to guess it was Asag.

Fen tapped my cheek with a claw and pointed to his wings. He made a flapping motion and then zoomed his one front leg around my face. He did it three times before I understood.

He would distract the beast.

And I . . . he touched me on the nose and made a scooping motion, as if picking something up.

I would get the mirror.

I was not a coward, but I was a child and fear

threaded through me. Fen cupped my cheeks and kissed me on the nose.

Remarkably, it helped.

I took a slow breath and nodded.

We couldn't waste any more time. He shot in first, while I pressed my back against the door. "Hey you big stupid lug, whatcha doing, doing?"

A quick look showed me that the giant had its back to me. Now was my chance. I shot in, and slipped on a pile of the snot that the giant had thrown at the door. I went down with a thud that turned its head my way.

"Whas is dis?"

Fen snarled and landed on the beast's head, raking his claws. "Hurry!"

I scrambled as the strange giant shrieked and screamed, reaching for Fen while trying to turn to me too.

Using the slick snot all over the floor to help, I slid across it to where the mirror sat in its own little holder at the foot of the giant. Literally the foot. The fat toes flexed toward me, as if he would claw at me, but at that moment Fen was really doing a number on the giant's head.

I scooped the mirror up, surprised at how light it was, and an alarm blared so loud it made even the giant howl.

Grasping the mirror tight to my chest, I bolted back toward the door. The door was sliding shut, from the top down.

"Fen, hurry!" I yelled as I dropped to my knees and bent backward, sliding under the door. Once more the giant boogies worked for instead of against me.

I spun on my knees as Fen shot through the thinnest gap, and then the thick door hammered shut.

Fen rushed to my side. "Are you okay?"

I looked him over. He had a tear in one wing and a gash on his side. "I'm okay, but you're hurt."

He shook his head. "Just a flesh wound, I'm fine." But he did climb to my shoulder, where he curled around and tucked his head against mine. His breath was coming in big deep pants. "Let's keep going."

I tucked the mirror under my arm and backtracked to the main tunnel. What were the chances that we were going to find a way into Asag's personal spaces? I didn't know, but I could hope . . .

Ahead of us a figure appeared out of the darkness, freezing me on the spot, until I saw who it was.

"Papa!" I ran toward my father.

He crouched and held his arms out to me. "My brave girl, so very brave!" His arms went around me but they felt strange, light. I blinked and looked up into his face.

"You aren't very solid, Papa."

His smile was sad. "No, I am not. But I am here to help you. Come. This way."

I put my hand in his and held on tight. "Papa . . . are you . . . gone?"

His fingers didn't loosen on mine. "Yes, my brave one. But there are others who love you."

"Zam." I bobbed my head. "She is coming for me."

He smiled down at me. "Zamira loves you, very much."

Warmth spread through my chest. "Will you go where Mama is?"

My father's face fell. "I hope to. You listen good to Zamira, now, yes? And you keep being brave."

He stopped in front of a section of wall that looked a little different. The stones were cleaner looking without a stitch of moss or dirt on them. "Here. This is a hidden path, all the way to Asag's quarters. I know what you seek. There is such an item there."

My father pointed at a tiny stone, a crescent moon etched into it.

"Fen, are you ready?" I put my hand over the stone, prepared to push it.

"I am," he rasped. "Your father is looking out for us."

"Your friend is hurt badly," Papa said. "You need to hurry. Get the item, and get to the main courtyard. You can do this, brave one. You must. For you are the one that Asag fears."

"I love you, Papa."

"And I will always love you, brave one. Go. I will watch and help if I can."

And just like that, my father disappeared. Gone. Just like Mama.

Tears leaked down my cheeks, and I brushed them away, then pushed the stone. It sunk under my fingers and a section of the wall opened up, just big enough that I could slip through.

On the other side, there were a set of stairs, and flickering lights. More glow worms.

I ran up the stairs, keeping my feet light, soft each time they landed.

Up and up and up we went.

I don't know how far I climbed before I stopped to have a break. I sat on the stairs and closed my eyes for just a minute. "Fen?"

He didn't answer me right away. "I'm here, little one. Keep going, I'm sleeping to reserve energy."

That seemed smart. But I was worried because it felt like he was leaving me. I bit the inside of my cheek and reached for Zamira. The way I'd reached for my father in the past. I didn't really understand how this worked, only that it did.

Zam wasn't far, not at all.

Her attention came straight to me, and I touched Fen, connecting the three of us at once.

Without hesitation, she sent a burst of energy into us both.

"Holy shit!" Fen shot from my shoulders. "That's like eating a bag of coffee beans!"

Without wasting time, I bolted up the stairs, Fen flying ahead of me now. My legs and muscles that had felt so tired just moments before felt light as a feather.

"Slow down," Fen suddenly whispered, and I looked up to see a door waiting at the top of the stairs.

Wooden, the backside where I stood had deep gouges in it, like something had been trapped down here?

Even as I thought it, there was the sound of claws on the stairs behind us. Just the slightest scrape, but it was there.

I bolted the last few steps and put my hand to the door. Only there was no handle.

"Fen, how do we get through?"

He touched the door all over. "I think it opens from the other side. Ask your papa."

Right, we had help, still. "Papa, you have to open the door!"

The scrabble of claws floated up to us along with a deep growl. I turned around to face whatever it was coming our way.

The beast below was thick-built but moved so quick up the stairs, leaping and bounding toward us. Its head was shaped like a block, wide open jaws and eyes that sparked green in the light. Its fur was thick, reddish, or maybe it had been white and was now stained with blood.

"Papa, help!" I screamed, not caring who might hear. Only knowing that we had to get through the door.

As the beast raced toward us, the door was yanked

open. I fell through and kicked at the door to slam it shut.

That wolf-ish beast hit the door, howling and scrabbling to get at me.

I lay back and stared up at the person who had opened the door.

He smiled, his mouth stretching wide in a way that I did not like.

"Hello, little kitten. Funny to meet you here."

CHAPTER
TWENTY-THREE

LILA

Zam's plan to have me fly up and spit acid on the chains to drop the drawbridge was a good one. The demons were behind us.

Asag ahead.

We had our little band of merry men, women, shifters and half demons to face them down.

But what Zam hadn't counted on, what I hadn't counted on, was Lilith making her damn move.

Zam stiffened suddenly and slumped forward as laughter that was not her own spilled out of her mouth. Well, shit.

"Maks, hold her!" I yelped as I shot away, toward the castle. Not because I didn't know what was happening. But because Lilith wasn't going to get Zam killed.

Lilith would in fact try to take out everyone else, though.

Sheer exhaustion nipped at the tip of my tail as I flew up and landed on the chains that would release the drawbridge. One on each side.

Shit, I hadn't counted on that either.

"In for a penny, come on acid," I said and then spit on the chains at my feet, using as little as I could, feeling the reserve in my belly sack empty. It wasn't like I could produce more on demand. I wasn't that kind of magic.

There was screaming and the clash of weapons below. More laughter.

Was this part of Zam's plan maybe? To somehow let Lilith take over? I struggled to see how that would help us, which meant my sister friend was in deep shit.

I flew to the other side of the drawbridge as it began to lower.

Asag was welcoming us in.

I danced across the chains, staying up high while I watched the bodies below.

Zam had Maks in her arms, her sword against his throat. Robert and Shem were facing them.

"If I kill him, your little spell ends."

"If you kill him," Robert shouted back, "Asag will end you on principle, you twat!"

The drawbridge suddenly let go on the one side where I'd spit acid, and it yanked itself free of the moorings, covering the lava.

Zam dragged Maks with her, across the drawbridge. His eyes shot to mine and I nodded. I already knew what I needed to do.

I flew away from them, locking onto Fen's energy. He and the kid were to get the mirror and the last item —whatever it was. I would bring them back to Zam.

To Maks, who would then do the spell thingy and Asag would be shoved back to the demon realm.

Call me crazy, but there were a lot of what-ifs still at play.

Fen's energy called to me and I followed it to a high tower and, thankfully, a window. While it wasn't open, I could see through to the scene playing out in front of me.

Reyhan was flat on her back on the floor. Fen was sitting on her chest, facing a huge man that could only be Asag.

Shit, shit, shit!

He was reaching for the girl, and she was clutching something.

The mirror.

I took a breath, back-winged so I was off the ledge and in mid-air, then shot forward, through the glass and into the room. I didn't slow, but went straight for Asag.

I hit him in the lower back and dug my claws and teeth in. Would it kill him? Nope. Would it distract him? You bet.

I let go of my bite hold. "Reyhan, shift!"

She did as she was told, and then she was just a tiny cub sitting next to a mirror.

Asag bellowed and reached back for me. I let go, spun around and grabbed the kitten up in my claws. "Fen, the mirror!"

"On it!"

"No!" Asag snarled and darkness filled the room so completely that it was if he'd plucked out my eyes.

"I can't see!" Fen yelled.

"Me either." I didn't know if Asag could see us.

"Papa, help!" Reyhan cried out.

Something wrapped around my upper body and tugged me forward, gently, so gently until I was out of the window and flying, looking down on the world.

A moment later, Fen appeared, and I saw what looked like Jasten ducking back into the darkness.

"Thank you, Papa," Reyhan whispered.

"Thanks, Jasten." I spun and flew away from Asag's tower. Fen was beside me, and our wing tips touched. I knew in that moment I could deny it no longer.

I'd found my mate. I looked across at him and he grinned at me. "I knew you wouldn't leave us behind."

I grinned back. "I thought about it."

A moment, just that one, and then we were all business. "Did you get the last item?" I looked down at the cub.

She shook her head. "No. He caught us first."

Well . . . that was going to make things complicated. "We'll figure it out. First, we need to get everyone out of here. Everyone."

"Will the mirror work anywhere?" Fen asked. "Shouldn't we need to be close to Asag?"

I shook my head. "I think that's why you need something of his. Right? That's how spells work."

As soon as I said it, I knew it was true. That was why the spell called for an item belonging to Asag. Something tied to him.

I flexed my claws, feeling the wetness there.

Asag's blood.

I grinned. "We got this. We just have to get everyone together. We can do it."

For the first time in the whole damn journey, I actually believed we were going to send Asag back into the demon realm. That we were going to make it happen.

Hope carried me forward.

But hope is not always the truth of things.

TWENTY-FOUR

ZAM

I was not surprised when Lilith surged forward to take hold of my body. I let her take control after a brief struggle. Layers and layers of plans, that was what it was taking to get us to this point.

I settled back and watched as Lilith yanked Maks from Balder's back, and stalked forward across the drawbridge. Watched as Shem and Robert followed, Robert cursing the hell out of Lilith.

Next to Maks I could see Roshawn standing, ready to take over.

He locked eyes with me. "You let her?"

"She needs to think she's winning. I need Asag to get close to us," I said.

"You don't think you can actually kill him, do you?" Roshawn's dark eyebrows shot way up. Way, way, up.

I smiled. "You think a raging, head-intact Asag will be easy to send to the demon realm? Or better that he's had his head removed and is somewhat helpless?" I laughed. "I might not be needed to make the spell work, Roshawn. But I can still help."

Because if there was one thing I was good it, it was wielding a weapon to kill a bad guy who thought he was a god's gift to the world.

Lilith stalked her way taking us both into the castle. A whoosh of wings and I could sense Lila, Fen and Reyhan circle back.

Shem took hold of Reyhan and held her close.

"Asag, brother! The time has come to free you!"

I snorted and lied through my teeth, making a feeble attempt to take control of my body again. "NO! You said that you wanted to kill him!"

"I lied," she whispered. "I would never hurt him."

"Brother fucker!" I yelled and flailed against her.

She laughed, and I settled back, carefully pulling on the energy of my family in the distance. I knew that it would tip Bryce off and that he'd likely come running, but this was it. We had to finish Asag now or never.

Really, I was banking on the now.

Behind us, Robert and Shem were doing something.

Prepping the spell, hopefully.

Ahead of us, darkness flowed out of one of the towers, not unlike the instabilismori demons only much, much larger. Ten times the size of one of them,

Asag rolled toward us, black fog spilling around him as he approached.

He stepped out of the fog, and I got my first real look at him, or at what he was presenting to the outside world.

His skull was shaved clean except that all over it were tiny spikes growing out of the skin. He was a muscle-bound brute, so big that I wasn't sure he even had a neck, and he walked with a bit of a waddle. Honestly, it was hard not to laugh at him.

I had no doubt he thought himself intimidating.

I thought he looked like an overstuffed penguin.

His orange eyes locked on me. Lilith.

"My love, what took you so long?"

She threw Maks toward him and Asag caught my mate around the throat.

Roshawn made a move and I hissed at him. "Wait."

Maks didn't fight. Not that he couldn't, but he didn't.

He knew the plan. "Let my family go, and I'll do the spell for you." Maks bit the words out.

Lila squeaked. "No, Maks, don't!"

Asag laughed and looked down at Maks. "Truly? YOU would set me loose on the world for your family?"

"Promise me you will leave them be, that they will all be safe and I will do it," Maks struggled to speak around the hold on his neck.

Lilith strode forward. "This body is lovely, don't you think?"

Asag looked her over. "I prefer you slimmer."

If my jaw could have dropped, it would have. Until he took the sword from her hands, and I was back in control of my body.

Asag stared down at me, his orange eyes lit up as he held onto Lilith. "I will never share my throne."

Fucking hell.

What a family of liars.

CHAPTER
TWENTY-FIVE

LILA

This was it, we were all going to die. I stared at where Asag held Maks, and now held up Lilith too.

Robert took the mirror. "Shem, I need a drop of blood from the girl."

Reyhan didn't even yelp as Shem took the edge of his knife and nicked her finger, squeezing out the blood onto the mirror's surface.

"The horn," I yelled.

Zam grabbed at her hip and tore the horn out, throwing it backward. Fen caught it and threw it to Robert.

"Roshawn," Robert said. "If you trust me, you can join me in this. I will let you do the spell."

I didn't seen Roshawn join into Robert's body. But suddenly he was gripping the unicorn horn hard.

Reyhan sat up. "You need something else. Something of Asag's. And the spell, I have it."

Asag roared and threw Maks away from him. Holding Lilith high, he launched at us.

Zam got in his way, dropping to the ground and tangling her legs around his so that he went to his knees.

The ground rumbled with his fall. "No, you will not banish me!"

Quick as the cat she was, Zam spun away from him, kicked his wrist that held Lilith, snapping the bones. I'm not sure if he felt the break, but his hand went limp and she snatched the sword away from him.

Still moving, she whipped the sword around, aiming straight for his neck.

And stopped, with the blade barely touching his skin. "Damn it, Lilith! Kill him! He'd have left you in the sword forever!" Zam screamed.

Asag stared at her. "Lilith, I would not have left you in the sword."

"Lies!" Zam yelled. "Lilith, we kill him now and then send you both back to the demon realm. You can fuck him or kick his ass, whatever you want at that point!"

The blade trembled. Asag didn't move.

"Here." I flew to Robert. "I have his blood under my claws."

Asag snarled. "I will kill you all."

"Maybe," I said. "But we're going to make you work for it!"

The mirror surface began to bubble and foam, and Robert set it on the ground. "The words of the spell, little one."

Reyhan cleared her voice and spoke.

"INTO THE VOID, *into the mirror*
Speak freely this, then speak it clearer
Demons lost, demons found
This demon here, must now be bound
Cast to depths, into the realm
This demon goes, and n'er is found."

ROBERT SPOKE THE WORDS, repeating them perfectly, then touched the unicorn horn to the surface of the mirror.

Asag screeched and flew upward, sliding into his less than corporeal form once more.

"Damn it to fucking hell!" Zam yelled.

"We need him here, to physically push him in," Robert said, his voice wobbling.

Maks had pushed to his feet, blood running down his neck. "Will it work?"

"It's not." Robert shook his head. "I need your body."

Maks ran to where the men stood, hunched over the mirror.

The castle was quiet, and I didn't like it. "What do you want to bet he's gone to get reinforcements?"

"I don't like betting against a sure thing," Zam said softly. "Something is wrong. Why isn't the spell working?"

"I don't know," Maks said, and I knew that Roshawn was in him. "We have all the pieces."

I didn't think Zam was talking to any of us, not really. Most likely she was talking to the damn liar, Lilith.

"She'll just lie to you again," I said. "Why even bother?"

"Because she was just betrayed by the one person she thought loved her better than anyone else," Zam said. "I know how that feels. Ishtar did it to me."

"Don't empathize with her," I said. "She's a liar. A demon. She has no feelings."

Zam nodded. "I know. But . . . unless we get some help, we're stuck at an impasse we can't survive. Asag will come back, with help. We have to make the spell work. Now."

TWENTY-SIX

MAKS

Staring at the mirror, he could almost see what was missing in the spell. Not unlike many that came into existence to counter a curse, there was an element of uncertainty—something more was needed that could never be spoken. Either the wielder of the magic understood or did not.

Roshawn did not. Master though he'd been, he only had his own memories and knowledge.

Maks, on the other hand, had more than enough memories and knowledge from all the Jinn masters to pull on.

"The glass must break through to the demon realm," he said, seeing the problem clearly, ignoring the noise around him. "We need something that will break the glass."

He tried a blade first: nothing. The spell pooled across the mirror and he could see the demon realm, but it was not touching this one. What would break through this spell?

What things would shatter it, or better yet . . . "Lila, you have any of your acid left?"

"A little." She flew to his shoulder and leaned over to get a look at the mirror. "Holy shit that's awful. Is that the—"

"Realm of demons, yes. And we must open this portal." He didn't want to think about what it would take to close it. A sacrifice, a life offered to seal the portal with blood and soul.

He did not mention that to anyone.

She leaned over and spit into the mirror.

The effect was immediate.

Sizzling nicely, the portal opened between the realms, only there was a single problem.

It was not big enough to shove anyone through. The mirror didn't change shapes.

"This is not good," he muttered and stood.

It was only then that he saw the demons. They rushed toward the castle, a veritable flood of darkness.

Even if they removed Asag, they would die under that wave.

Unless . . .

Maks ran to the edge of the drawbridge. "I hope I am not wrong about this."

CHAPTER
TWENTY-SEVEN

ZAM

T stared as Maks stood over the edge of the drawbridge and dropped the mirror.

Did I trust him? Completely.

Did I know what the fuck he was up to? Not a clue.

I will not kill my brother.

I stared at the sword in my hand. "Fine. Maks, want to tell me what you're doing?"

"One-way portal into the realm of demons." He pointed into the lava.

Lilith shivered in my hand, fear slipping through her.

I looked over the edge, down into the moat that moments before had indeed been lava. Now? Now it shimmered and danced like oil, and through the oil were scenes out of my nightmares.

Lurching, hulking beasts, a blasted landscape, the dull throb of a dying sun.

"That's a nope from me." I took a step back, feeling the tingle of something behind me.

I spun as Shem shouted a warning.

The black mist that preceded Asag wrapped around our entire group, sucking the heat away along with the remaining light.

Blinded, I went very still. Reaching for my connections to my family, I felt them around me. "Drop," I said.

The trust in me was a hundred percent. Each one of them got low, so when Asag moved toward me, I swung hard and true, landing a blow directly to him.

His bellow ripped through the air and Lilith screamed with him.

I didn't want to hurt him!

"Too late, Lilith, I heard you tell me you yearned to kill him!" Had she ever said that? Nope.

I knew though that once she and Asag were back in the realm of demons, they could fight it out.

The mist blew away and Asag was on his knees. I didn't hesitate, just swung again, straight for his neck. He grinned up at me. "She won't cut me."

I had no breath to answer because I was already moving.

And when Lilith fought the swing, I stepped around, changing my stance and the power in my arms.

Her blade went halfway in, sticking against his vertebrae.

He garbled up at me, as I yanked the sword free.

He was on his hands and knees, injured but not dead, he head hanging loosely.

Worse though was that I could see the black shadows around him pulling his head back on.

"Fuck!" I knew what I had to do, but . . . damn it all.

"We've got things here," Lila yelled. "You get him in the damn moat!"

I stepped back and through the doorway in my mind, and let my body slide into my jungle cat form.

There was immense pain, but I had to do it.

This was the only way.

Lilith was a part of me now.

No, no!

Her screech said it all. She knew he was done. And she would be the one to end him.

TWENTY-EIGHT

REYHAN

Everything was happening so fast. So fast. The man who held me, held on a little tighter as Zam fought Asag.

"Don't worry, I won't let them hurt you," he said softly to me.

A shiver ran through my body and I looked up into his eyes. Eyes that flashed a quick red before settling back to amber.

Demon. This one was a demon.

I screeched and he clamped a hand over my mouth. I was still in my cub form and I used everything I had to get free of him, but he held me tight and forced me to watch.

"You see, there must always be a balance," he rumbled, and then laughed. "If she can beat my son, then he was never meant to be the leader here, but then I must take something from her. Someone that she values as much as if it were her own child."

I couldn't move.

Asag was on the ground, and Zam had shifted into her jungle cat form. Slashing and biting at Asag, she took hold of his head and yanked it free, then tossed it across the courtyard. Lila and Fen helped it along until it rolled into the moat.

Then without any hesitation, Zam dragged Asag's remains toward the castle moat.

The man holding me, Shem, cleared his throat. "I would not do that if I were you, Zamira."

She had Asag by the hand, held between her teeth as she turned to look our way. Her eyes narrowed.

"So. You took Shem?"

The man chuckled. "I did. I found it amusing to take him over and see how quickly you trusted him, how stupidly you let him along for the ride."

Zam shook her head. "I'm done playing games."

She ran toward us, and the man threw me. I let out a wail as I went flying across the space, toward the lava. Only it wasn't lava, it was a moat full of a portal to the demon realm. I didn't have wings.

But I had friends who did.

I was caught up by Fen and Lila, and yanked clear of the portal.

Asag's body was beginning to move. "The beast!" I yelled as I shifted, landing on two feet. I ran toward him and grabbed his hand, yanking him toward the portal I'd just been saved from.

Fen landed beside me and shifted into his larger form. "Here, let me."

He grabbed the body and threw it into the portal.

The black wave of demons hit the edge of the moat and spilled over. Maybe they weren't bothered by lava, but they didn't realize right away that wasn't what they were crossing.

They were sucked down into the portal, and a whirlpool started up, drawing them deeper and deeper.

"We need a sacrifice," Maks said. "Someone has to give their life to close it."

"No!" Zam was running toward him, and tackled him to the ground. "We promised each other, we aren't being separated again."

I wrapped my arms around myself. "Papa, what do we do?"

I felt my father near me. "You stay right where you are, brave one. You have done your part. Now it is time to let the grown-ups figure the rest out." He pressed his lips to my head and then was gone.

He was right, I was tired, and there was nothing more I could do.

CHAPTER
TWENTY-NINE
SOLEIL

S oleil watched from the top of the tower. Zamira and the others had not needed her, not once.

But now they did.

Asag had underestimated the girl and her family. She found herself smiling as she stared down at her only son. He had a chance here, in this world. But it would mean closing the gate.

Swooping down, she flew over the body Nico had stolen and yanked him free from it. "Come, love. It is time to go home."

Nico writhed. "No! No, we are free here!"

She didn't hesitate, but instead kept swooping toward the portal. Her wingtips brushed against Zamira's head and the jungle cat looked up. "Throw the sword in the portal. Then I will close it."

Zamira did as Soleil asked, shifted to two feet and promptly passed out. There were no others strong enough to carry the sword and not be affected, except perhaps one. She looked over at the little girl.

"Take the sword, little cat, and toss it into the portal."

Green eyes flashed as they narrowed. "You aren't lying?"

"No, I am not."

Robert—her son's new name which she rather agreed with—bobbed his head. "You will make the sacrifice?"

"I will, for you to have a life now, free of these monsters."

"And you will have an eternity with them as the price." His voice was thick. He was a good boy.

"I will be fine."

She reached out and touched his face as Nico fought her hold with her other hand. "If I can tell you one thing, I can tell you this. You survived this fight because none of you tried to take the glory. Each of you had a part to play, each of you had a role to fulfill and that is why you succeeded where all others failed. Well done."

The child had picked up the sword and dragged it to the edge of the portal. She plopped it in with a little skip in her step. "Feels fucking gross."

Soleil couldn't help raise her eyebrows. "Such language."

The child grinned up at her. "I'm no lady, I say fuck."

THIRTY

ZAMIRA

The thing was I woke up with a pounding headache, but I was warm and safe because I could feel both Reyhan and Lila snuggled up with me under a blanket.

"Where are we?" I mumbled.

"In the castle." Reyhan sat up. "I threw Lilith into the portal, then the angel lady swooped in after! You were totally asleep and so you didn't see the spray of colors that went up into the air like a rainbow and all sparkling and all the demons were so angry! It was so pretty and then Robert said he had to go, and Shem asked where the fuck he was and how did he get here, and Maks said not in front of the little one, but then I reminded him that I am no lady, just like you and that means I can say fuck if I want."

I put a hand over her mouth. "Hold up. You mean we won?"

"Fen is out with Maks and Shem, and I think your brother too, opening all the dragons' cages," Lila said. "I told them to go and that I'd come get them if anything changed with you. But I was pretty sure you'd just passed out, like the last time you shifted too often."

I made myself sit up. Because I felt like we were missing something.

"Lila . . . what about the golden dragon?"

Lila shot up. "Oh. Shit."

Which is how we ended up searching the castle. No weapons. No magic with the exception of the tiny droplet I still had humming in my hand. What the hell good was it now? The fight was over and the magic had done nothing.

My hand warmed even as I thought that.

I grimaced, but there was no one in my head to bitch at me. No Lilith screaming away, and I found myself sighing. It was a relief to be done with her and that weapon.

"This looks like a grand hall." Lila pointed with a flick of her tail.

The doors were solid gold and Reyhan clutched my fingers a little harder. "Is it safe?"

"Probably not," I said softly. "But seeing as none of the challenges were even real, I'm not concerned. Other than the fact that this dragon shifter was probably a friend to Asag."

"I AM NO SUCH THING!"

The voice was booming and it stopped us at the doorway. Lila peeked in first. "Oh . . . it's safe, come on."

I shoved the door and followed her in. Reyhan stayed close, and I could feel the tension in her. She was going to need a long time of quiet and rest after this.

The room was indeed the throne room, or what passed for one. The room was trashed, furniture broken to bits and the sound of a chain slithering around. A small waterfall spilled into a pool, which then fed into a nice stream looped through the room. I stepped over one of the tributaries, noting the sparkling silver fish. More than that, though, my eyes were drawn to our quarry.

Chained to the throne, the golden dragon was.

But he was hardly the threat that he'd been made out to be. I remembered him from the dream where I saw Mamitu, Pazuzu and Gorg talking. He'd been smaller than them by quite a bit. And that translated into a very, very small dragon.

Smaller than Lila.

"Get this chain off me! Before Asag comes!" he howled and flung himself about. His golden scales were covered in filth; I supposed they might have been pretty at some point.

"Hold on, before we do." I held up both hands, palms facing the little guy. Sure, he was small, but he was still a dragon. "Asag is dead, the demons are gone and we're letting all the dragons go."

The small golden dragon's jaw dropped. "For real?"

"She is not a liar!" Reyhan snapped and took a swing with a well-placed kick that sent the golden dragon tumbling.

He came up hissing and a pitiful amount of smoke popped out of his mouth. That was it.

"I didn't exactly like the guy. He strapped me in here after promising me a world of freedom and riches!"

I looked at Lila. "What do you think? Set him free?"

She looked around. "Nah, he has a supply of fish in that pond over there." She pointed at the water running through the room. "I say leave him. He can find his own way out. I'm betting he's not even a proper dragon shifter."

"You are a queen, you cannot leave me!" he begged, scrabbling toward her. "I have suffered for a long time, I have learned my lesson."

That paused Lila and she looked over her shoulder. "Swear it on the skin your body carries, on the smoke in your belly, and the wings on your back."

Reyhan curled tighter to me and I picked her up. She dropped her head to my shoulder. "I don't think he's bad. Just scared."

I nodded. "But it's not up to us what happens to him, but to Lila."

"I swear on my skin, my wings and my fire that I

will do no harm to this world. I only wish to be free of this place." He bowed his head and a shudder ran through him. "I have taken no form but this one in all this time, I am not sure I will be able to shift again."

Lila grunted and walked over to the chain, and spit up a bit of acid on it. No unicorn horn needed after all. Just another lie. "Then you are free to go, but I will keep track of you."

The golden dragon, Gorg was gone in a flash. No laughter, no noise, nothing.

Lila tumbled into the closest stream to make sure that her acid was cleaned off, then she flew to me. I caught her with my free arm.

"You think that we will get our magic back?" she asked quietly. "I'd have thought that . . . maybe when Asag died that the magic he stole from us would be free."

"We'll search the castle," I said. That was all we could do and now we had the time.

WE SPENT three days searching the castle and freeing the last of the living dragons. They left together in a herd, flying west toward Dragon's Ground.

"Do you want to go with them?" I asked Lila. She shook her head.

"Even now, they would not accept me, Zam. And I'm okay with that. I played my part, I helped you save them. And now there will be no more thefts of the eggs."

The one thing we couldn't find sealed the deal for Lila, I was sure of it.

There was no vault, there was no hidden magic. Maybe Lilith knew all along then that I'd been trying to fool her? I'd never know with her gone. I would be grateful for that little fact.

But no magic for us meant . . . well, it meant not much changed, to be fair.

Bryce and the rest of the Bright Lion Pride arrived and helped us search. The unicorns had all fled after Balder had sent them away. I knew why—to stay clear of Asag, once they understood he'd want them too.

What was left of his father's horn, I offered Balder. "What do you want me to do with it?"

He sniffed it all over and then touched my saddle-bags with his nose. Keeping it was fine by me; who knew when you might need a magical artifact.

As we rode through the demon city, we found no demons at all. The people that were left outside the city of Trevalon were few and far between.

"Most were demons," I said softly. "They smelled like it anyway. Asag must have put the call out he needed help."

The streets were strangely quiet. We rode through slowly. Reyhan slept a great deal—she'd been through a lot.

. . .

A WEEK later we reached the market where Maks had had to sell Batman.

The black gelding saw us and whinnied right away, pushing on the gate with his chest. Even at a distance I could see that his leg was sore. He might not make the journey back.

"You . . . I am surprised you actually came back," the trader said. She was young, and feisty looking. "I kept him as promised. Your money is still going to his feed. You want me to keep him longer?"

Maks shook his head. "No, keep the rest of the money. I'll take him with us now."

He let Batman out of the paddock and the old gelding hurried over to Balder—who promptly squealed and nipped his friend on the shoulder. As if it were Batman's fault for being left behind.

As we rode away, Reyhan asked to ride Batman. Maks set her on his back and the gelding happily trotted ahead with her.

"What do you think was so special about her?" Maks asked suddenly. "Why Reyhan, of all the shifter cubs, why her?"

It was a question that had been burning in my mind. "I don't know. Maybe we'll never know."

Maks was silent for a few minutes. "I wish we still had Robert to ask."

On cue, there was a whoosh and who the hell should appear, but our friend Robert. "What is it?"

My jaw dropped. So did Maks's. "What the hell?"

"No, rather I avoided hell when my mother took all of our places in order to seal the portal. But what question do you have?"

"Two, actually," I said quickly before I forgot. "Why Reyhan, of all the cubs, and all the shifters? And where the hell is our magic?"

Robert smiled and patted Balder's neck. "Well, that's really the same question and answer, if you want to know. Reyhan's mother . . . is not a shifter. She was an elemental spirit. Very special. Very rare. She carries the blood of the lost in her. And with that power, she carries your magic. She is the vault. She is the one that held your magic, until it poured out of her and into the mirror."

Yup, jaws dropped again. "So it's gone?" Lila whispered. "Really gone?"

Robert shrugged and tugged his long cloak around him. "Gone for now. I would think that if you want to find a way back, that the gifts that were once yours could be once more."

We traveled in silence for a few minutes. "Thank you, for your help. For saving Lila," I said.

Lila bobbed her head. "Yes, seeing as Toad was completely oblivious."

"I was dealing with Roshawn . . ." He paused. "Who I haven't seen since."

"He's with me." Robert grinned. "I figured as we were old friends, I could take him along until he decided he'd had enough of this world. We've already checked on Vahab. He's happy where he's at. Thinks he's going to rule the Storm Keep." Robert shook his head.

"At least he's happy," I said. I found my fingers going to Mamitu's ring and then handed it to Robert. "I think that you should take this. You knew them. I don't know if they were helping or not, I . . . there were so many lies, I can barely think past them."

Robert took Mamitu's ring. "Yes, the past is murky, and the present clear. I hope that they were helping. Pazuzu disappeared. I think perhaps he was more with Asag than he let on."

That had been my thought too. "Fare thee well, Robert. Try not to unleash any more demons on the world, okay?"

Robert laughed and pulled his cloak higher until I saw the wings for what they were. "Who said I opened the portal?" His blue eyes twinkled and I shook my head.

"A good guess. Your mother said you were trouble too."

He leapt up and curled into a somersault, disappearing from sight, but his laughter took longer to fade.

"We would not have made it without him," Maks said.

No, we wouldn't have. But Soleil's words about Robert's role in setting Asag free told me that he had a debt to pay, which he and his mother had done.

. . .

WE DIDN'T FIND Jasten's body, but we held a ceremony for him once we reached the desert. I held Reyhan as she cried and promised her she would stay with me and Maks. With Lila.

"I know that," she whispered. "My papa told me that you loved me, that I would be your little girl now."

With my throat tight I held her closer yet. "Yes. You're mine now, brave one."

Maks crouched beside us. "And mine too."

Lila popped her head in against Reyhan's cheek. "Sisters."

Fen laughed. "And a brother now too."

For the first time in I didn't know how long, my family felt complete. Maybe we'd had to come all this way, just to find Reyhan? Was that why I'd felt the need to keep going?

I let myself feel where my feet wanted to go and knew that it was west. Home to the Oasis, my family, and my roots.

I stroked a hand over Reyhan's head. "Are you ready to go home?"

She grinned up at me. "Yes."

I looked at Maks. "Are we done adventuring for a while?"

"For my life, yes." He leaned over and kissed me. "I would like to sleep for a week and then discuss how we can keep you two from trouble." He pointed at me and then Lila.

Fen laughed. "Don't look at me. Where she goes, I follow. So, if it's trouble, then I'm there."

Lila butted her head against his. "That is my home of love; if I have ranged, like him that travels, I return again."

Maks grunted. "I don't know that one."

I grinned. "I do."

He kissed me again. "I'm sure you do, my brilliant mate."

We stood and the five of us looked out to the west where our home waited. I mounted up on Balder, and Maks went to Dancer. Reyhan leapt up with me, shifting into her cub form so she could curl in my arms.

"It is a race then?" Maks asked.

I looked at the Bright Lion Pride ranging around us on horses that were just horses. "No, it's not. Besides, we have an old friend to go find."

UP NEXT!

Not sure where to go next after finishing this series? Check out my website for my other series www. shannonmayer.com

OR if you can't stand leaving Desert Cursed, Zam, Lila and Maks behind, check out my merchandise store, www.mayersmerch.com for some amazing swag like this . . .